Saint Milburga's Bones

Jason Vail

Saint Milburga's Bones

A Hawk Publishing book.

Cover illustration copyright canstockphoto.com.
Cover design, map of Ludlow Castle by Ashley Barber

ISBN-13: 978-1514701928
ISBN-10: 1514701928

Hawk Publishing
Tallahassee, FL 32312

Saint Milburga's Bones

Saint Milburga's Bones

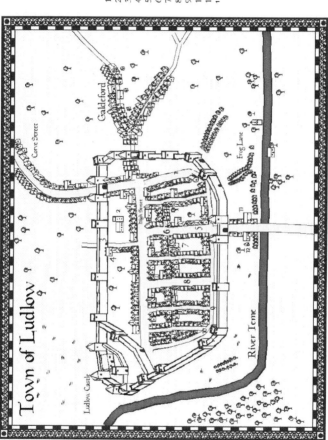

Town of Ludlow

Galdeford

Corve Street

High Street

Frog Lane

Ludlow Castle

River Teme

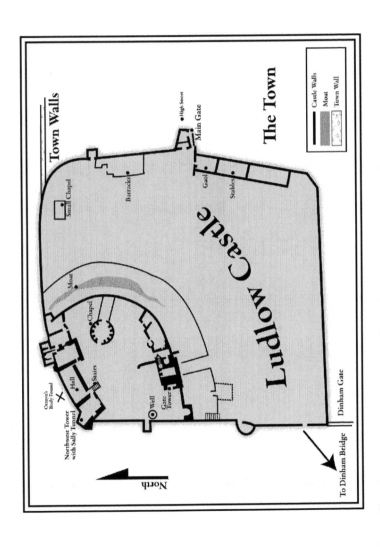

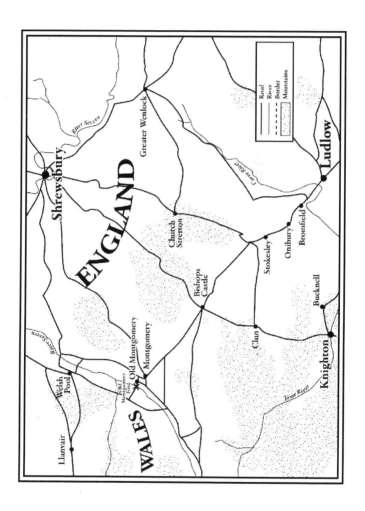

Saint Milburga's Bones

MARCH 1263
to
APRIL 1263

Saint Milburga's Bones

Chapter 1

Harry the beggar did not ordinarily pay much attention to the doings of the Broad Street gang, a collection of the younger, unapprenticed boys from the families living on the street up from his station at Broad Gate. They had long since learned not to pelt him with dirt clods or shower him with taunts, so that mostly they left each other alone.

But this day as the boys slipped through the gate around a cartload of cordwood so as to be out of sight of the gate warden, Gip, Harry heard them muttering excitedly about a dead man they had just seen. One of them said distinctly, "We got to show Dick!"

Another of the boys noticed Harry watching. "Shut up, idiot!"

Corpses were as common as fallen leaves, but the mention of this dead man caught Harry's attention. Perhaps it was because a castle guard had disappeared without a trace a few days before; perhaps it was because the boys were not allowed by their parents to leave the confines of the town walls. The intersection of these two circumstances provoked his interest.

"You there!" Harry put down the block of wood he had been whittling. "Come here!"

The boys stopped and stared at Harry in amazement. They were not accustomed to being summoned by beggars, and by Harry in particular. The leader of the group, a boy of eight called Nate, recovered from his astonishment. He called back, "Screw you, asshole!"

"If you don't get over here now, I'll have Gip tell your mother what you've been up to," Harry said. "Sneaking out of town without permission, and God knows what else."

Nate hesitated. "Who says we don't got permission?"

"If you had permission, you wouldn't be sneaking back in. Now get over here."

Nate sauntered across the street, trailed by his fellows. "What do you want?"

"What's this talk about a dead man?"

Nate shuffled his feet. He frowned, then his brow cleared as he had a thought. "If you show us your stumps."

"You've seen 'em already."

"Not up close. And we get to touch them."

"You'll have to wash your hands first. I don't like people rubbing their grubby hands over them. I'm a clean person."

This claim provoked laughter, since Harry among all the beggars of the town was known to be the most filthy, although to everyone's surprise he had bathed last month and suffered a shave and a haircut which new growth only now had begun to erase.

"Our hands are clean enough."

"No, you've had them in your mouths and in the dirt, and God knows where else. Wipe them off at least, for God's sake."

There was nothing around which was suitable for wiping except the boys' shirt fronts, which had to do in this circumstance. They knelt before Harry as he drew back the blanket that normally covered his stumps except when he wanted to impress those who might be inclined to add to his begging bowl. One of the boys rested his foot on Harry's wooden platform, which he sat upon to keep himself out of the dirt and which had rockers on the bottom to make it easier for him to get around by the use of his hands. The platform pitched forward. Harry batted the foot away.

"God!" one of the boys marveled as he touched one of Harry's legs. "That's horrible! How did it happen?"

"In the wars," Harry said, which was a lie. His legs had been cut off after a wagon had run over him and they had gone gangrenous. The surgeon had been quite proud of his work, since few people survived a single amputation let alone two at once.

"Did it hurt?"

"Not a bit," Harry lied again, for it had been the worst pain he had ever experienced. "Now about that dead man."

The boys exchanged looks as if waiting for one of the others to answer. Finally, Nate said, "There's a dead man by the castle. Under the north wall."

"What's he doing there?" Harry asked.

"He wasn't telling nobody."

"Don't be so sure about that," Harry said. "Dead men can talk. You know that coroner fellow, Stephen Attebrook?" The boys nodded. They all were familiar with the dark-haired knight who often walked with a limp. "You should find him at the Broken Shield this time of day. One of you run up there and tell him about this dead man. He'll want to know about it. Dead people are crown business, you know. It's treason not to tell him."

The boys looked worried at the possibility they might be charged with treason for not reporting this dead man.

Nate nodded. "I'll go." With an anxious glance through the gate at Tad Thumper and his gang, who were tormenting a robin with a broken wing, the boys ran up Broad Street.

The formidable Edith Wistwode, matron of the Broken Shield Inn, blocked the door when the boys tried to enter. She was known to be swift with a clout when crossed, so Nate kept well clear as he stated the nature of their business. Mistress Wistwode crossed her arms and straightened up, her face softening. She sighed, "There's never an end to it, is there? Sorry, boys, he's at the castle. You'll have to seek him there."

The boys perked up at this, since it raised the possibility of getting inside the castle, where they were not allowed. The thrill was compounded by the fact the place was full of knights and soldiers who had come to attend Prince Edward, son of that feckless king, Henry III, who had arrived only a few days ago intending to continue the war against the Welsh which had begun during the winter.

The gate wards at the castle listened to their request to see Sir Stephen and dashed the boys' expectation of further fun. One ward said, "If this is some kind of tale to get in, you've another think coming."

"It's true. We saw him," Nate said.

"By the wall?"

The boys all nodded.

The wards exchanged worried looks. One who had spoken first said, "I don't like the sound of this."

"You don't think it could be Ormyn?" asked the other.

"I hope not." The ward rose from his stool. "I'll be right back."

"I hate to say it, Stephen," said Sir Geoffrey Randall, "But I don't think you'll be of much use."

When Stephen Attebrook had heard that his superior, the coroner of Herefordshire, had answered the commission of array with three knights and fifteen archers, he had hurried up to Ludlow Castle hoping Sir Geoffrey would take him on as a fourth knight. Although he had feared this answer, an outright rejection was dismaying. He had lost part of his left foot to a Moorish axe in Spain the previous year, and now the only work he could get was as the coroner's deputy. It was low-paying, a demeaning position for a knight who was used to better, more prosperous times. He tried to keep a straight face.

Randall, heedless of the hurt he had inflicted, went on briskly, "Your foot, you know. With half your foot gone, you can't ride properly. Not enough left to put in the stirrup. Just a stump from what I'm told." Stephen had never discussed his infirmity with Randall, or with anyone else in town for that matter, except for a close circle of acquaintances, yet somehow the whole world knew about it.

"I can use a lance, despite the injury," Stephen said. But Randall was right that he had trouble keeping the foot in the stirrup. "I handled Nigel FitzSimmons well enough." Last fall he and a shadowy knight named FitzSimmons had fought a duel across the river in Ludford which he had managed to win.[1] The outcome had in fact been close, but it didn't help to tell the whole truth.

"Yes, yes, but that was just a joust. Any fool should be able to stay in the saddle for that. What about the melee? How will you handle that? A man who cannot stand in his stirrups is useless in the melee. You know that as well as I."

"Well, what if I asked to be taken on as a scout?"

"A scout? That's for the light horse," Randall scoffed, as if the notion of Stephen riding with the light horse, who were mainly Welshmen who happened to own a pony, was absurd .

Or perhaps, Stephen thought, the prospect reflected badly upon Randall: it would not do for his protégé to be seen riding with Welsh rabble, some of whom had already begun to go barefoot despite the fact that it was still March and cold. Stephen was sorry now that he had brought any of this up. Randall had really been his only true chance. He could not go to others and ask for a place. They would wonder why Randall hadn't taken him on; there would be inquiries, and then his deformity would be more widely known than it already was, and he would be ruined for good, with no possibility of advancement.

Before Stephen could say anything further, Randall shouted at the servants erecting his tent. One of them had not secured a corner line and the whole thing had begun to sag, the center pole leaning precariously.

"You should get in there and help right that thing," Stephen said sourly to Gilbert Wistwode, Randall's clerk, a round little man who was also watching these proceedings.

"I am not an erector of tents," Gilbert said. "I am a man of the mind. I leave such work to those more fit for it. You know, it wouldn't hurt for you to use your head now and again. Instead of rushing forward."

"Thank you, Gilbert. Your advice is noted."

---

[1] See *The Wayward Apprentice.*

"If you'd only take it. But you are young, and the young are ever foolish. You knew he would refuse, didn't you?"

"I hoped there was a chance."

"Hope . . . we need it so, but it can lead to wishful thinking, which often leads us astray." He knitted his fingers upon his belly.

"Is it Sunday? I don't see a pulpit."

"No need to be so testy. I am only trying to help."

Just as Randall's servants righted the tent pole, one of the gate wards came round the side of the tent. He spotted both Randall and Stephen at the same time, and seemed torn about whom to approach. He stepped up to Randall, as the senior person.

"What is it, Bert?" Randall asked, not wanting to be distracted from the business of the tent.

"My lord, there's been a report of a death," the gate ward said.

"A death? How inconvenient." Randall waved at Stephen. "Tell my deputy. He'll take care of it."

"Duty calls," Gilbert murmured as Bert crossed the few steps separating them from Randall.

Bert the gate ward stood back with his companion ward as Stephen listened to the boys report their find.

"By the castle wall, you say?" Stephen asked. "Where?"

Nate pointed toward the north. "That way."

This was not helpful, so Stephen said, "Show me."

The shortest way around to the north side of the castle, which occupied the northwest corner of the town, was through Dinham Gate, which gave access to the town from the west. Beyond the gate, Nate turned north along the wall forcing everyone to clamber at the base, for the ground here sloped enough to the River Teme that there was no ditch. They passed a small round tower that had only been built a few years ago, then a square one that did not jut out from the wall, which marked the boundary of the inner bailey. This was followed by another square tower and then a third, larger one, where the castle wall curved east. As the group came around this third tower, Nate halted. He pointed to a spot ahead about halfway between this tower and the next.

"He's down there," Nate said.

By down there, he meant some distance down slope. The hill was overgrown with brush, hazel mostly, which had not been cleared as it should have been last fall during the previous emergency when people feared Ludlow might be attacked. The presence of the brush made walking along the slope difficult, so Stephen proceeded close to the wall, peering through the branches for some sight of the body.

At last, he came upon it.

"My, my," Gilbert said. "That's not what I expected."

"Indeed," Stephen said, as he knelt by the corpse.

The dead man lay on his stomach. He was stark naked.

Stephen turned the body over. The underside, including the face, was blue and crisscrossed with darker marks that had the appearance of the crushed grass beneath him. He said, "Ah, poor Ormyn."

"You know him?"

"One of the castle garrison. He's the one who went missing day before yesterday."

"I heard about that. Just disappeared during his watch in the night, or so they say."

"Well, now we know where he went."

"At least he doesn't smell too badly."

"That is a relief." Stephen glanced up at the wall. They were about halfway between the two rectangular towers on the north side of the castle that stood on either side of the great hall. "Most likely he fell from there."

"You think he fell?"

"How else did he get here? None of the gate wards saw him leave." As Stephan looked up, he noticed that many of the hazel branches overhead appeared broken. They could have been snapped by Ormyn's body.

He turned Ormyn on his side. His long brown hair fell back from his face, and Stephen saw that Ormyn's left ear had been split almost in half. He peered closely at the wound. There were bits of bark within it and in abrasions along his cheek. Stephen lifted the hair, which had a few twigs in it as well. There were more abrasions on his neck. Now that he paid more attention, he could see bruises along his back, mainly on the left side of the body. He turned the body onto its back and bent his face close, looking for similar marks on the front. There were none, until he got to the dead man's face. Near the edge of the mouth on the left side was a puncture. Stephen put a finger in the man's mouth and drew the lips aside. Ormyn's teeth were crooked and one on the jaw at the left stuck out a bit. There was blood on the inside of the mouth and a corresponding puncture. All this seemed consistent with a fall through the hazel.

"If we could blame the wall, Sir Geoff would be very pleased," Gilbert murmured.

"It is a very costly wall, isn't it?" The law required that the instrument causing a death must be valued and that the hundred where the body was found fined the value of that instrument, which had to be paid by the people of the hundred.

Stephen clambered up to where Nate and the other boys were waiting. "That's how you found him? Naked like that?"

The boys shuffled their feet, eyes on the ground. "Yes," Nate said.

"Did you touch him?"

"No."

"How did you know he was here?"

Nate equivocated for a moment. "Somebody told us."

"Who might that be?"

Nate's hesitation went on longer at this question. "Tad Thumper."

"Tad Thumper?" Stephen repeated, as his mind sought the implications of this revelation. Tad Thumper was one of Will Thumper's great brood. Will was a thief and a bully, quick to fight and often hired when someone needed a thumping for such things as the failure to repay a debt, hence his name.

"Yes," Nate said, looking worried now that he had said Tad's name. His anxiety was understandable. Tad was as much a bully as his father. He and his gang of urchins had the town boys terrified.

"How did Tad find the body?"

"I don't know. He didn't say. He charged us a full penny to see it."

"A full penny? Where'd you get a full penny?" A full penny was quite a lot of money. Many men didn't earn so much for a day's labor.

"My father gave it to me."

There was something about the way Nate said this that told Stephen he was lying. More likely, Nate had stolen the penny. Stephen hoped that he had stolen it from his father rather than somebody else. In any case, he dropped that line of inquiry. Thefts weren't within his purview, and he didn't want to get involved.

Gilbert climbed up beside Stephen. "Well, you have to admit, it's rather enterprising of young Tad."

"Although unlawful."

"I don't think the law means much to the Thumpers."

"I got that impression the last time we ran into Will."

"I suppose I should fetch the jury. Although I doubt they will be able to make much of this. You'll remain?"

Stephen nodded. "You boys, get out of here. And say nothing about this to anyone. Understand?"

With a chorus of "Yes, sir! Yes, sir!" the boys backed away and scampered around the corner of the western tower.

"I say, I wish I could move that quickly," Gilbert said. "But I'm getting old."

"You could never move that quickly."

"I have moved quickly enough in the past to save you from disaster. I shall be right back."

Saint Milburga's Bones

As Gilbert followed the boys' track through the tall grass, Stephen sat down. He daydreamed that he was riding at the head of a squadron of horsemen heading into battle as he had done in Spain before he had lost everything. But that would never happen again. He was stuck where he was, dealing with the dead.

Chapter 2

The view north from the castle was pleasant even at the base of the wall, and, having exhausted his capacity for day-dreaming, Stephen amused himself as much as that view allowed while he waited for Gilbert to return with the jury. He had often enjoyed this view from higher up. A great meadow spread from the slope, bounded on the left by the River Teme and the right the suburb of Linney, concluding at the line of trees marking the stream of the River Corve, which fed into the Teme. In ordinary times, the meadow served as the pasture for the horses of the castle garrison, but now it was filled with the tents of the army the Prince had summoned so that he could continue the war with the Welsh. Smoke from numerous fires hung over the tents, sharing the air with distant voices — one set of singers making a carol whose harmony was quite good, and another distant set of singers so inharmonious that anyone close by might be moved to plug his ears; a woman shouting at a fellow over the fact he had urinated on the side of her tent; and a shoemaker boasting of his skill.

Stephen grew restless when more than an hour passed without any sign of Gilbert or the jury. He rose and stretched — and nearly fell. His bad foot made standing on the slope difficult. As he tottered to regain his balance, he heard voices on the wall above, other men of the castle's standing garrison, including the watch commander, Ralph Turling.

"Sir Stephen!" Turling called. "Your man says you've found Ormyn Yarker! Is it true?"

"I'm afraid so."

"Where is he?"

Stephen pointed to where the body lay beneath the hazel. "There."

"I can't see anything."

"He's there."

"Dead then?" Turling asked.

"Yes."

Turling turned away and spoke to someone whom Stephen could not see. A woman appeared trying to pull herself up between the crenellations to get a look for herself, but men of the garrison pulled her back.

"Be still, Bridget," Turling could be heard to say. "We'll take you down straight away. Come now."

The figures went to the tower to the right, and presently the men and the woman Bridget came around the corner at the base of the wall. Stephen wondered how they got out of the castle so quickly, but then he remembered there was a little used underground sally port from the western tower that emerged in a small grove of trees down slope.

Bridget had to be Ormyn's widow, although Stephen had never seen her, nor had any idea what she looked like, since he had not involved himself in the lives of the men of the garrison. She slipped by Stephen and worked into the hazel. She was much younger than he had expected: no more than sixteen or eighteen, with straw colored hair and satiny skin, young and quite pretty, in fact. Ormyn was in his thirties at least. But then it wasn't that unusual for men to marry much younger women, particularly the second time around.

She knelt by the body. Stephen followed her, prepared to advise her not to disturb Ormyn since the jury had not yet had a chance to look at him. That warning was unnecessary.

Bridget sat on her heels and looked at the body without any expression of grief. She sighed, "That's it, then, thank goodness."

Turling glanced up at the top of the wall. "I suppose he fell off."

"Seems a likely explanation," Stephen said.

"Taking a piss, probably," Turling said with some disgust. It was not unusual for men on the night watch to pee from the battlements, since, strictly speaking, they were not allowed to leave them to go to the latrine. The practice was undisciplined and risky, but the leadership could not put a stop to it. One solution was to leave a basin in a tower, but

Turling did not approve of this and had removed those put out by the previous commander. He thought such basins gave the watch an excuse to huddle in the tower.

"Hard to say."

"His drawers aren't down?" That was how men killed by such falls were usually found.

"Someone got to the body before we found him. Stole all his clothes."

"He should have had a sword, shield, and spear. Those are missing as well?"

"I'd say that whoever took his clothes and boots probably got those too."

"It's such a pity. I've had better men, but he was dependable, never late with a mouthful of excuses and never asleep on his watch." Turling kicked at a tuft of grass. "He volunteered to take another man's watch the night he disappeared, too. What bad luck. Now three children are fatherless."

The mention of the sword, spear, and shield got Stephen thinking. He should have considered the possibility already that they might have fallen apart from the body and could still be somewhere in the brush. "Can you have your men search for Ormyn's spear and shield?" Stephen asked. "They might still be here."

"Good idea," Turling said. He called to the five men who had come down with Bridget to start a search along the wall in the vicinity of the body.

The men fanned out along the base of the wall and began forcing their way through the bramble, as Stephen and Turling descended to Bridget's side.

"Come away, Bridget," Turling said, hand on her shoulder. "Let the coroner do his business. Then you can have him back."

Bridget nodded, as she climbed the slope to the wall. She squinted to the top. "It's hard to believe he fell. You know how good he was at climbing."

Stephen remembered this too, now that she had mentioned it. Last autumn, shortly after he had arrived at Ludlow, Ormyn had climbed the outside of the east tower of the inner bailey to the highest window on a wager, getting his purchase from no more than the crevasses between the stones. When Ormyn reached the top, he had shown off with a handstand at the brink of the parapet.

Meanwhile, the search party had been making a great deal of noise as the men worked their way about the space between the towers until there was a shout by the eastern tower. "We've got 'em!"

Stephen climbed up see what they had got. Three of the soldiers came toward him bearing a shield painted green and yellow, and a spear.

"The shield's Ormyn's all right," the soldier bearing it said. "You can see his mark here." He held turned the shield so that Stephen could see the inner side, where there was a ¥ in black paint above the grip. Ormyn had been illiterate, like most men, although he knew enough to be able to recognize and to write the initials of his name.

"Show me where you found them," Stephen said. "The exact spot."

"Over there," the soldier said, pointing at a place about ten yards from the body.

"Take me there. The exact spot, I said."

The exact spot proved to be closer to fifteen yards than ten, in Stephen's judgment, and the spear was found almost twenty yards away.

When Stephen returned to Turling and Bridget, the other two soldiers who had searched toward the western tower had also come up. One of them was sniffing at the contents of a tin canteen. This struck Stephen as out of place, since he did not remember any of the soldiers having a canteen. It was not the sort of thing a member of the watch was allowed to carry for fear they might keep ale or wine.

"What have you got there?" Stephen asked.

"Found it yonder," the soldier said. He pointed toward the west tower.

"Let me see."

The soldier reluctantly surrendered the canteen. As well he might. It was new, with hardly a scratch on it, the leather of its strap new as well and still a bit stiff. Canteens like this were worth a bit of money.

Stephen sniffed the contents. "Ale. Not gone all sour yet, if I'm any judge. Show me where you found it." He had no idea if that detail might be important, but Gilbert would insist on knowing and he didn't want to come up short when he was asked about it.

The soldier led Stephen back another twelve or fifteen yards, down into the slope, and halfway up the other side. "It was there," he said, "at the base of that hazel. Just lying there. Odd to find such a thing lying hereabout, ain't it?"

"It's been a day of oddities," Stephen said. "No reason we can't have one more to add to the confusion."

"Can I keep it?"

"No." At the soldier's frown, Stephen added, "Not until we sort things out and see where it fits."

At last Gilbert showed up on the path at the foot of the slope with not merely the six men of the jury, but also a cart. The jurymen listened to Stephen's report, and briefly questioned the soldiers about the finding of the spear and shield. Then they climbed up for a look at the body and its wounds.

"Well?" Stephen asked. "What is your verdict?"

"What I can't understand," Thomas the tanner said, rubbing his round nose, "is why he'd lug that spear and shield to the wall. You've been in castle guard, sir. Is that something a fellow in his position would do?"

"No," Stephen said. "He'd leave them on the parapet."

"And then," said Philip, a glover, "there's the fact they were found so far from the body. If he'd fallen with them, they'd have been found nearby, don't you think?"

There were nods all around.

"It ain't right," Michael, a baker said. "It ain't right, at all. Something's fishy. Do you even think he was taking a piss?"

"I don't know," Stephen said. "It's the spot for it, if someone was of that mind. The hall's up there. It's the one place where a man cannot be seen from the bailey. So he could have."

"But you don't think he simply fell," Gilbert murmured.

Stephen shrugged. It was the jury's decision about how Ormyn died. He could influence it, if he wanted to. But he wanted to see what the men made of this evidence.

"Seems like he might have been helped," Thomas the tanner said. "But it's hard to say, ain't it? A bit ambiguous."

"Ambiguous," Philip said. "That's a word too big for you."

"Oh, shut up."

"I'm in favor of a verdict of murder, more probable than not," Michael said. "What do you say?"

"That sounds about right," Philip said.

"You've got some more work to do, sir," Thomas Tanner said with a grin. "Too bad it don't pay."

"That has been an ongoing problem," Gilbert said behind Stephen's back.

A corpse attracts crowds as well as flies, so there was a great collection of people anxious for a view as the cart entered the outer bailey. They were disappointed, however, because the body arrived covered with a blanket and remained that way, even after the jury released the body to the family and the cart was led away to the little chapel in the outer bailey that served the garrison.

"Well," Gilbert said, "there's nothing like a dead man in the morning to wake one up. What do you say? Shall we tell Sir Geoff the good news?"

"That there's no fine? He'll surely be thrilled to hear that. He's impatient enough as it is with what little I've managed to take in."

"That's not entirely your fault, although you could channel the discussions more than you do."

Turling fell in beside them as they wended through the tents erected in the outer bailey toward the one belonging to Randall. "They're saying its murder. Is it true?"

"It looks that way," Stephen said.

"That's impossible."

"Where murder is concerned, little is impossible in my experience."

"He was an amiable man. He had no great debts that I know of. He quarreled with no one. You know that. You knew him. What could drive someone to throw a fellow like him from the wall?"

"Perhaps he jumped," Stephen said, thinking of Bridget's lack of grief. He sensed trouble in their relationship. If it didn't erupt into murder, suicide was not unheard of. "Unhappy people have been known to do that."

"No! I refuse to believe it!"

Stephen glanced at Gilbert. "I've been faulted before for overlooking every possibility."

"He has," Gilbert said. "Overlooked other possibilities, I mean."

"It is not a clerk's place to criticize his master," Turling said.

"Of course not, sir."

"He says that now," Stephen said. "You should hear him when he gets me alone."

"I don't know why you put up with that," Turling said, as they arrived at Randall's tent.

"He was forced upon me," Stephen said. "I have no authority over him. Besides, he's my landlord. He thinks that entitles him."

"Merchants," Turling said, turning away. "Always thinking themselves better than they are."

"We're not actually merchants," Gilbert said when Turling had gone. "We're innkeepers. We don't sell things."

"People like him don't know the difference. Besides, you sell food and a bed. Those are things. It makes you a merchant. And if this was a bigger town, you'd have your own guild. Perhaps you should start one."

"I never thought of it that way."

"And I am setting you right, for a turn."

"Better not let my wife find out. She thinks she has the exclusive right to do so."

"Edith thinks that about everyone."

"She is difficult sometimes — uh — I didn't say that."

"And I didn't hear it."

A servant informed them Sir Geoffrey had gone to the inner bailey to attend Prince Edward, so they crossed the drawbridge to the square gate tower to the inner portion of the great fortress. Where the outer bailey was broad and spacious, the inner bailey was small and cramped. There were only a handful of buildings here: a kitchen, round and belching smoke; a well house; a stable; and a round chapel which seemed to have been dropped down almost in the middle without much thought. Despite the fact the chapel, stuck out in the bailey like a wart on a man's nose, the Genevilles, who owned the castle, were quite proud of it, and had richly decorated the interior, which one could not miss since you had to walk past the entrance to get to the hall, and the chapel's doors were kept open in all but the worst weather.

There was a swarm of activity within the chapel, none of it stately, quiet, or measured as befitted a chapel. People were standing around throwing their hands about in argument, or with worried expressions. The tall figure of Prince Edward could be seen at the altar rail, his hand on a stooped cleric's shoulder, urgently questioning him about something. Stephen stopped to gape, wondering what could have brought the Prince out of the hall at a time not normally given to Mass.

Randall was in the crowd and came to the doorway at the sight of Stephen and Gilbert.

"Sir," Gilbert said, as a fellow Stephen recognized as Wace Bursecot, a goldsmith's journeyman carrying a small box of tools, squeezed around them in a hurry to be away, "we've come to report about a murder."

"Never mind that now," Randall said. "Something worse has happened."

"And that is, sir?" Gilbert asked.

"The Earl of Arundel's relic of Saint Milburga has been stolen."

Chapter 3

Arundel's relic of Saint Milburga . . . it took a moment for Stephen to adjust his mind. He had not been privileged to see this relic, although he had heard about it. Few, in fact, were allowed to see it. Gilbert had described it as being kept in a jeweled box that had a glass top that most of the time was concealed beneath a wooden cover. Even pilgrims who had paid to be in the presence of the relic were often not allowed to see it. Yet people came to the relic not so much to see it, but to receive the good luck that was said to arise from prayer before it. Percival FitzAllen, the earl of Arundel, had required that the monks of Greater Wenlock, a Cluniac priory twenty miles to the northeast which was founded by the saint centuries ago, to bring it to Ludlow so that the Prince could behold it.

"So what?" Stephen asked. "Why is that our concern?"

"Good Heavens!" Gilbert gasped. "That's terrible! Who would want to do such a thing?"

"That's what everyone wants to know," Randall said, answering Gilbert's question. "Vanished from its box. It is a dark day, a dark day indeed. What shall we do now? The relic is gone, it's blessing taken from us. Already there's talk that it's a bad omen for the army, and word's not even got out of the bailey yet."

"The theft's just been discovered?" Stephen asked.

"Only a moment ago."

"It disappeared from its box? A locked box?"

"It did indeed. As if into thin air."

"Well, I'm sorry about the relic," Stephen said. He almost added that he was not sorry about FitzAllen's loss, but prudence stayed his tongue at the last moment.

He didn't see any point in remaining here if Randall did not want to hear about Ormyn. He looked around for Walter Henle, the castle's constable and the sheriff's chief deputy in this part of Herefordshire. He had to be in the crowd but

Stephen could not spot him. Henle would want to know about Ormyn.

Stephen was thinking about going inside when the crowd came to him, headed by Prince Edward and the aggrieved party, Percival FitzAllen, with the stooped cleric who had to be the prior of Greater Wenlock Priory.

Randall, Stephen, and Gilbert backed away to allow Edward to pass. The Prince paid no notice to Stephen or Gilbert, but FitzAllen looked at Stephen with hatred. It seemed that FitzAllen had not forgotten his grudge against him.[2]

Edward paused. "Sir Geoffrey, I understand that you have a candidate for sainthood buried in your church cemetery."

"That is true, your grace, although some doubt that she is really a saint."

"But there are claims that she has performed miracles."

"Her remains, my lord. She was found dead on at the door of Saint Laurence's just last winter. A few who touched her before she was buried claimed to have been healed by her grace. Lately some others have repaired to her grave site and come away whole. Or so they said."[3]

"You sound skeptical."

"My current duties require the exercise of skepticism, my lord. I am afraid that it becomes difficult not to doubt in other things."

"Ah, right. You are our coroner here. You must be careful about that. There are some things that we are not allowed to doubt. I should like to go to this woman's grave. Rosamond . . . wasn't that her name?

Randall glanced at Stephen for help. Stephen nodded. Randall said, "Yes, my lord. That's what some people have taken to calling her."

"Perhaps she will give us guidance about what to do in this calamity. If you would show me the way, I would appreciate it."

---

[2] See *A Dreadful Penance*.
[3] See *The Girl in the Ice*.

"Certainly, my lord, but I think you know the way."

The way to Saint Laurence's church was straight down High Street from the castle, and the church was hard to miss, its brownstone tower looming over its neighbors. Like the castle, it was an anchor to the town.

When he first arrived, the Prince had been a great novelty. The entire population had turned out and crowded the streets when the Prince appeared. But after a week of his coming and going on this visit or that, or on a hunting or hawking trip, the novelty had worn off, so that the Prince, at the head of a large gathering, since he could not go anywhere without one, only attracted a glance or two, and none of the journeymen or apprentices in the High Street shops broke in their work to come out and gawk. The Prince did not seem to mind, since he never paid much attention to common people except when they got in the way.

Although Randall was supposed to be leading the Prince to the church, Edward soon outdistanced him, even though Randall's gout had subsided so that he could walk perfectly well for a change. But Edward was just a bit taller than Stephen, who was six feet in his stockings, and moved quickly upon muscular legs that tight hose showed off quite well. Even FitzAllen, who was a big man, seemed small beside him so that when Edward spoke to FitzAllen, sometimes he had to bend his head with its jutting chin, auburn hair falling about unshaven cheeks, to FitzAllen's ear. Stephen was too far back to hear what they were saying, but FitzAllen looked back at Stephen and said something, at which Edward looked back at him, too.

"Poisoning Edward's mind against me, no doubt," Stephen said to Gilbert, who was hurrying to keep up with the rapid pace Edward set.

"Why would you think that? You're too small a man for a Prince to bother with, although it's a measure of your worth that you are hated by great men rather than little ones," Gilbert puffed. "How many is that now? Two ? Three? You have been so busy that I've lost track."

"I haven't been counting. More, I think, if you include Henle."

"Oh, he's no more bother than a fly. I wouldn't count him."

It did not take much time for Edward's long legs to bring him to College Lane, and the procession swept around the corner to the churchyard. Edward passed through the gate in the stone fence and turned to Randall. "Which one is it?"

"That one, over there." Randall pointed to a stone about four feet high topped with a Celtic cross. A Welsh stone cutter living in the town had made it after his daughter had been healed of a mass of boils by having the grass growing over Rosamond's grave rubbed on them. The monument had been there only a couple of weeks, but people had chipped off pieces of it to take away as relics so that the corners looked as though they had been nibbled by mice.

Edward knelt on the grass before the stone. This forced everyone in view to drop to their knees as well, regardless of whether they had any intention of invoking the aid of the putative saint. He remained there quite a while. Although kneeling took the weight off Stephen's bad foot, it began to twinge sharply.

At last Edward rose. He walked toward the church door. "Around here, then? That's where she was found?"

"Yes," Randall said, hastening to the Prince's side. "Right where you are standing."

Edward was standing in the middle of the path, which was not where Rosamond's body had been found. As best as Stephen had been able to work things out, she had died just outside the church door and then someone unknown, although he suspected her husband, Warin Pentre, had dragged the body to a place just off the path a few steps away from where Edward stood. But he did not correct Randall.

"And people walked over her after the snows came," Edward marveled. "And they didn't even know it."

"It is quite a story, your grace," Randall said.

"Yet she was found."

"By a beggar. On Christmas Day."

"And did that find bring him good fortune?"

"I believe it did, your grace."

"I have prayed that she will bring me good fortune, both for the return of Saint Milburga's relic and for the army in the war to come. We will need her help, since Saint Milburga is beyond our reach at present . . . unless . . ."

There was a pause which Randall, who had some experience dealing with royalty, did not venture to fill.

"Unless someone finds the relic for us."

"I'm not sure I follow you, your grace," Randall said, although Stephen suspected that he followed very well and did not like what was coming.

"Percival would like to have his relic back," Edward said. "And so would I. Coroners are experienced in solving mysteries. What could be more mysterious often times than the manner of a man's death? And I understand that you have considerable skill in that department. I would like you to find the relic, and return it to its rightful place."

"But, your grace, you will need every fighting man you can get in the coming weeks. We are likely to be outnumbered, and a single knight left behind could spell the difference between victory and defeat."

"Yet the relic is more important than a hundred men, even a thousand."

"Well, there is one man who can be spared for this task. A man who perhaps will be more useful in such an endeavor than I."

Edward glanced at Stephen. "Yes, I've heard that you have a deputy who has proven to be rather resourceful. But he and Percival apparently have a history, and not a friendly one. Are you certain he can be trusted in this to use every effort, even though it may benefit a man he dislikes?"

"I think that overstates Sir Stephen's feelings, your grace."

"Well, let's hear from the man himself. That's always better, don't you think, than getting things second hand?" Edward beckoned to Stephen. "Come here, fellow!"

When Stephen didn't move promptly, Gilbert gave him a little push.

"Your grace," Stephen said as he bowed to the Prince. "How can I help?"

"You've heard what's been said," Edward said. "You know our problem. Can you find Saint Milburga's relic?"

"I can't make any promises, your grace. You can never tell how these things will turn out." Stephen looked up into Edward's eyes. They were gray, and they seemed at odds with his manner, which was bluff, with heartiness that some might misinterpret as fecklessness. The eyes were distant, measuring, holding back, like the eyes of a certain lady he knew, cold, weighing the world and all who passed before them, searching for weakness and for how one might be useful. He wondered if he would ever see the lady again.

"No, I don't suppose you can. If you find the relic, you will be richly rewarded. Percival will see to it, won't you Percy?"

"Well, your grace . . ." FitzAllen muttered.

"Oh, very well, Percy, we will pay half the reward. Will that do?"

"Thank you, my lord."

"There now. Can we count on you, Sir Stephen?"

"I will do my best, your grace."

"Off you go, then." Edward turned away toward High Street.

The procession followed Edward out of the churchyard, leaving Stephen and Gilbert alone by Rosamond's stone except for Percival FitzAllen, who lingered by the gate.

Stephen rested his hand on the stone, thinking of the dead girl who lay beneath it. Only he, Gilbert, Harry, and one other knew who she was, and she had not been a saint but just an ordinary girl fleeing a tormented life. He would not have wished the manner of her death on anyone: a sad accident, and the waste of two lives full of promise.

Gilbert tugged his sleeve. "Come on. You can't do any good here."

"So now we have to waste our time for no purpose?"

"We?"

"You don't think I'm doing this without you!"

"I was afraid that you might take that position," Gilbert said.

"You've often claimed that you are the brains behind my success. It's time you proved it."

"I shall be glad to, especially in this matter," Gilbert said as they reached the gate and FitzAllen. "It's too important to be left to the likes of you."

"Don't think that this changes anything," FitzAllen said.

"You have such a winning way," Stephen said. "I am underwhelmed. Are you going to send more of your boys to kill me? I'll have a hard time finding the relic if I'm dead."

"We will have a truce. For the time being."

"Truces are good. Tell me about this relic. What does it look like?" Stephen did not think that even Gilbert, who was well informed about spiritual matters, knew this.

"It's the thigh bone of the saint. It's broken in two about the middle, like a snapped twig."

"What color is it?"

"How would I know?"

"You've seen it, of course."

"Brown. I think it's brown. You've seen old bones before. It doesn't look any differently from what you'd dig up there." FitzAllen waved at the graves behind them.

"A brown thigh bone broken in two. There aren't many of those around England, are there Gilbert?"

"I should say not," Gilbert murmured with an odd reserve.

"Don't think about substituting some cast off," FitzAllen said. "There are emeralds affixed to each piece."

"That should make it easier to spot. I am curious. Why would you bring such a valuable object out of safekeeping into the middle of an army?"

"My intentions are not your concern."

"It seems to me that everything about the relic is now my concern."

"I will not have you inquiring into my purposes. They are none of your business."

"Thank you, my lord earl. You have been most helpful." Stephen extended his hand. "Shall we shake hands and confirm our truce?"

"I'll not shake hands with the killer of Warin Pentre," FitzAllen spat.

"I am not responsible for Pentre's death," Stephen said, choosing his words carefully.

FitzAllen snorted. "What rot! You were seen at the same house where supporters of Simon de Montfort gathered for a secret meeting. Then you turn up at Pentre's castle, you depart a short time later, and the next thing we know, a hostile army of Montfort's people attack and burn it. It's too much to be a coincidence. You were sent there to spy him out, to find out his weaknesses so that the others could enjoy success. But I'll tell you what — if you find my relic, I'll not denounce you as a traitor. Yet, anyway. *That* is my part of the reward."

FitzAllen spun about and strode up College Lane.

Saint Milburga's Bones

Chapter 4

"He left out a lot of what happened," Gilbert said as they stood in the street watching FitzAllen vanish around the corner.

"Probably because he doesn't know it," Stephen replied. "But he knows enough to hang me."

In November, Stephen had indeed slipped into Bucknell, where FitzAllen's retainer Warin Pentre maintained a castle. His objective was two-fold: to determine whether Pentre was linked to the deaths of some merchants on the Shrewsbury road, and to confirm that Pentre was behind a series of barn burnings and raids on the lands of supporters of Simon de Montfort. He had found both suspicions to be true at great cost to himself. Stephen said, "I should go."

"Go? Go where?"

"Away. Somewhere away, where I'm not known. Where I can change my name, if necessary, and make a new life. I'm done here. FitzAllen will see me ruined in the end."

Gilbert took Stephen's arm and they walked toward the corner. "That would be the prudent thing, I suppose. It's a shame. Edith will miss you."

"I think Edith regards me as someone who needs to be cleaned up after and who takes up a bed that could be put to profit."

"Well, there is that. But she still likes you."

"She doesn't often act like it."

"You misjudge her. She's quite fond of you, I swear it. If you must flee, I suppose Lady Margaret would take you in, and help you find a place. Although it will be a matter of great distress to find you formally allied with the other side."

The Lady Margaret de Thottenham occupied an uncertain position among Montfort's supporters, who were opposed to the king and the men closest around him and whom everyone expected would rise in rebellion soon; an important spy, or something. Stephen wasn't exactly sure. It had been her

38

townhouse in Shrewsbury that FitzAllen had referred to. He wondered if he should warn her that she might have been found out. "I suppose she might."

"You might at least want that reward before you go."

"What? FitzAllen's silence?"

"Well, I think the Prince has something more substantial in mind. God knows, you could use the money. I doubt you've got more than half dozen pennies to rub together at the moment. Why, if money doesn't suit you, you could confess your part in Pentre's demise — claim you were duped or something, you have the face of someone quite dupe-able, so he might believe you — and beg for a pardon. The Prince wants that relic returned very badly. He wouldn't have promised a reward himself otherwise."

"And how likely is it that I'll see any reward?"

"You've been lucky so far. It could turn out well."

They reached the corner of High Street and turned toward the castle.

"Waste of time," Stephen said.

"Probably, but you never know." Gilbert tapped his temple. "But remember, you have my keen mind behind you."

"That is a great comfort."

"Come now, you could at least sound like you meant it."

"I did mean it. If I cannot convince you of that, how am I going to convince Prince Edward that I'm not a traitor, when I really am?"

"You shall have to work on your delivery. Just copy how the great lords dissemble. But you'll have time for that. It's not like we're going to find this relic in a day."

Stephen and Gilbert reached the castle gate and entered the outer bailey. He slowed as if measuring the tents filling up the enclosure almost to bursting in order to gauge how to get through them, but he was really buying time to think about what to do next. He didn't have a firm idea. Whatever success he had enjoyed in the past came more from blind luck than any shrewd plan, though he was weak enough to accept credit which he did not feel he deserved. He had hoped that Gilbert's great mind would provide helpful suggestions, but he seemed to be out of them at the moment.

"I think we should talk to the prior," Stephen said. He was certain that the stooped cleric he had seen in the Genevilles' chapel was the prior, as the monks had not yet departed.

"Of Greater Wenlock Priory?" Gilbert asked, stopping short.

"What other prior did you think I was referring to?"

"I suppose you expect him to tell us who was the last person to see the bauble and all that."

"Bauble? You're making light of this important relic?"

"If it had been up to me, I'd never have fastened gems to it. I don't understand how they could have let it be mutilated like that."

"Perhaps you should ask the prior, if it troubles you so much."

"I think I'll let you ask the prior." Gilbert started to turn away.

Stephen caught his arm. "You're not coming?"

"It just occurred to me that one of us should report to Henle concerning Ormyn's death."

"Well, I'll admit that needs doing, but we have to pass the chapel before we get to Henle. He can wait until we question the prior. Come along, let's get this over with."

Gilbert did not register any more objections, but Stephen still practically had to drag him into the inner bailey.

"What has got into you?" Stephen asked as they reached to door to the chapel.

"Nothing. Nothing at all. I think I'll wait here. I'm sure you can handle this bit by yourself." He slipped to the side so he could not be seen by anyone still in the chapel.

Exasperated but unwilling to drag Gilbert bodily inside, Stephen left him skulking about the doorway.

The crowd that had gathered at the discovery of the missing relic had broken up and wandered off, and only the castle's priest was in the chapel in conversation with a half dozen monks in black habits. They fell silent as Stephen stopped nearby, waiting for them to finish whatever they had to say to each other.

"May I help you?" the priest asked.

"Father, the Prince asked me to look into the matter of the missing relic, and to find it if that is possible."

"And you are?" one of the monks asked. He was a striking man in his forties, with a long Norman face. He was as tall as Stephen, which meant he was taller than the others. His eyes, which regarded the world with an aristocratic detachment, lingered on Stephen's worn blue shirt with its patched elbow and fraying cuffs, his stockings with a new hole just below the knee, and his battered boots.

"He is our coroner, Brother Adolphus," the priest said, "or rather our deputy coroner, Sir Stephen Attebrook. He's proven to be quite adept at finding things, principally having to do with murder."

"Perhaps he should apply himself to finding a suitable living," Brother Adolphus said. "I've seen bricklayers who looked more prosperous."

"Be careful what you say, Brother Adolphus," Stephen said, stung at the insult. It was hard enough, in his misfortune, to have to endure the looks of people like him. To have it brought up out loud was harsh indeed, especially since it was the truth.

"Or what?"

"Easy, there, brother," said the prior of Greater Wenlock, an elderly man whose back was stooped as if he was carrying an invisible weight, with only the cane clutched in his knobby hand preventing him from falling. He fumbled with a gold chain around his neck that supported a wooden cross. It had got tangled with a thong that held something out of sight beneath his robe. "There is no need to be so sharp. Sir

Stephen has only come to us to do his duty, as our Prince has given it to him."

"I am sorry," Brother Adolphus said, although to whom he was sorry was not clear.

"Please pay no heed to Brother Adolphus," the prior said. "He is upset over the disappearance of our precious relic of the saint. It has much disturbed him, as it has disturbed us all. I so dread returning to our brethren with word that what they entrusted to our care has been lost. They will not forgive us."

"How was it lost?"

"My, you have a direct way, don't you. We don't know, actually."

"How could you not know?"

The prior sighed. "Perhaps you should see for yourself while you hear our story. Please come this way, if you would. I am Brother Anthony, by the way."

Most chapels were small and square. This one was large and round, due perhaps to some conceit of the Genevilles. Within the confines of acceptable taste, every magnate strived to be different in his display of wealth and power. There was an extension at the rear that reached as far as the eastern wall of the bailey. Stephen had never been inside it and had no idea what to expect, since it had been added after he had been here as a boy squire. Stephen thought the prior would lead the way, but the priest, Father Theophilus, headed the procession without being asked to do so, although Brother Anthony set the pace at a quick hobble.

Across the north side of the extension were a series of chambers, while the south was open and sunny. In ordinary times, it appeared to be a library, for there was a shelf of books and what could be rolls of accounts running the full length of the open chamber, and a scriptorium or clerk's office. Two writing desks were now crammed in a corner and a good part of the room taken up by cots.

"Who sleeps here?" Stephen asked.

"We do," Brother Adolphus said.

"You, the monks of Greater Wenlock?"

"Who else did you think I meant?"

Brother Adolphus was rapidly rising to the top of the list of people Stephen most wanted to strangle. People were not usually so openly rude, mainly because among his sort open rudeness provoked violence. Perhaps Adolphus thought Stephen would not dare to take open offense. Stephen was no more accustomed to suffering such insults than Walter Henle might be, but for the sake of his inquiry, he held back a sharp retort. It was too bad Gilbert wasn't here so he could get credit for it.

"We keep, or I should say, kept, Saint Milburga's bones in there," Brother Anthony said, indicating the third chamber on the left with his cane.

Stephen lifted the latch and pushed the door open. "You did not lock it?"

"Of course, we locked it," Adolphus said. "There's no use locking the door now that it's gone."

Stephen went in. The chamber appeared to be a storeroom for vestments and other implements used in religious services: a staff, caps, platters for the bread, and vessels for communion wine. Under the window high above the reach of even the tallest person was a large old trunk. It did not seem out of place in here. Brother Anthony came round Stephen to stand by the trunk. He flipped up the latch and opened it. He removed a smaller box and set it on the closed lid of the trunk.

"We kept the relic in here," Brother Anthony said.

Stephen knelt by the trunk. The small box was painted a cheerful red and the sides were reinforced with bronze that had been polished so diligently that it shined even in the dim light of the chamber. It lacked the glass top he had been told to expect. The box's most significant feature, however, was the padlock and set of bronze hinges that secured the lid. The hinge had been pried loose from the box. The marks from the tool used to do so were plainly visible on the wood.

"Do you mind?" Stephen said, reluctant to open the box without permission.

"You have our permission," Brother Anthony said.

Stephen lifted the lid. A bed of red velvet of a shade matching the paint on the exterior lay within the box. A depression in the middle indicated where the relic had lain. Even though the light was dim, he saw what appeared to be splinters of wood upon the velvet. He bent close to examine them. He picked one up, ignoring the sharp intakes of breath behind him. It was a sliver of bone. He laid the sliver upon the velvet. He was about to close the lid when a tiny object wedged between a fold of velvet and the wall of the box caught his eye. He dug down for it. It was small and round and had a hole in the middle. He had no idea what it might be. But one thing seemed clear: it was made of gold. He thought about returning the little round thing to the box where he had found it, but some instinct caused him to put it in his belt pouch. He closed the lid, and stood up.

"So, you kept the room locked? At all times?" Stephen asked.

"Yes," Brother Anthony said.

"When was the last time anyone saw the relic?"

"Oh, it was three days ago. The day after we arrived."

"Was it normal to keep the relic in its box and not to gaze upon it?"

"It is a powerful object, my boy. We do not lightly trifle with it. It is brought out only at special occasions, and those of need."

Stephen looked up at the window. The shutters were closed, as anyone would expect. But the latch securing them was not fastened, if the unbroken line of sunlight at the boundary between the shutter panels was any indication.

"And the theft was discovered today, when the Prince came to see it?" Stephen asked.

"Yes," Brother Anthony said. "I am afraid so."

Stephen was about to say that he had seen enough when there was a commotion at the door. Two black-robed monks had someone by the arms. One of them said, "Brother Anthony! Look whom we found!"

"Why, Brother Gilbert," said Brother Adolphus. "We wondered where you had got to. Tell, us, where is that Gospel you stole?"

Chapter 5

"I — I — I —" Gilbert stuttered. "I took nothing that belonged to the priory when I left. Except for myself. I am guilty of that."

"We stopped caring about your disappearance years ago. But along with you, there was a manuscript missing," Adolphus said. "A copy of the Gospels."

"I don't know about any such thing!"

"The coincidence is compelling."

Stephen pretended to study the box that had held the relic, as if he had no interest in this conversation.

Anthony looked from Gilbert to Adolphus. "I must sit down. This is one too many shocks for my heart for a single day." He hobbled toward the door.

Gilbert and the other brothers backed into the common room to allow him to pass. Anthony sat on one of the cots with a groan.

"I am sorry to see you in this state, brother," Gilbert said.

"The penalty of living so long." Anthony wagged a finger at Gilbert. "I may be infirm, but my mind is still clear as a bell. Now, tell us what you have been up to these many years." His eyes wandered to Stephen, who had come out as well. "Is our business concluded, sir?"

"Not yet," Stephen said.

"Ah, what more can we do?"

"This man works for me. Your business with him is with me as well."

"For my part," Anthony said, "I only want to rest and reminisce about old times, and to hear his news."

"A charge has been laid," Stephen said. "A charge of theft. It is a serious matter. Either Brother Adolphus must stand behind it and be prepared to offer proofs, or it must be withdrawn. What proofs do you have?"

Adolphus' mouth was a thin line. "Just that shortly after Gilbert left us, that copy of the Gospels was found to be missing."

"Shortly after?"

"A day or two. Little more. Gone from its cupboard where it had been hidden."

"A day or two? So anyone could have taken it, then? Rather like this relic."

Adolphus' mouth opened and closed.

"You will have to do better," Stephen said. "Come along, Gilbert. If Brother Adolphus has nothing more to say, we are finished here."

Stephen went out with Gilbert upon his heels.

"So Greater Wenlock was your priory," Stephen said when they reached the relative safety of the bailey. "You never said."

"There never seemed to be a reason to." Gilbert rubbed his cheeks with the palms of his hands. "It was long ago. Another life, almost."

Stephen walked around the chapel to the north wall of the extension. "I recall seeing a copy of the Gospels in your possession. You showed it to me once."

Gilbert sighed. "I copied it myself, every letter. A little bit each day, mostly during the evening, when I was supposed to be sleeping."

"Don't monks belong to the priory? Everything you make belongs to the others. And you used the priory's pen, ink, and parchment, I have no doubt."

"I did."

"Doesn't that give Brother Adolphus grounds to think the book belongs to the priory?"

"It was my labor that made the book! I meant to pay it back. But I've been afraid to return. I am so ashamed. I was weak. I could not live up to my vows. I yielded to temptation. I could not bear to confess my failure."

Stephen knew what that temptation had been: Gilbert had fallen in love with Edith, as plain-looking a woman as you could find anywhere, but beautiful to him. Stephen knew the power of such temptation. He had loved a woman once, a Jewish girl in Spain, with more intensity that he had ever thought possible. He had been happy for the only time in his life. Then illness had taken her away, leaving despair and sorrow that had not diminished despite the passage of a year.

"Anyway," Gilbert said when his confession met with silence he took as disapproval, "if you must know, I took the book away to finish it. I could not leave the work undone."

"You did, eh?" Stephen said, mouth moving and finger pointing as he counted the windows on the north side of the chapel annex so as to identify the one belonging to the room in which the relic had been stored. He stopped beneath the window that he thought should be the one, which was about halfway between the round chapel and the wall of the inner bailey, where wooden steps led up to the wall walk. Like all the other windows, it was twice a man's height above the ground, tall and narrow, but wide enough for a man to fit through if he could climb high enough to reach it. "Here we are, I think. And did you?"

"Did I what?" Gilbert asked, distracted by the counting.

"Finish it."

"I did," Gilbert said with some pride.

"How did you manage such a feat? Do you have the Gospels memorized?"

"Some of them, but I copied the rest from the books at Saint Laurence's church."

"No one there thought your work odd? I mean, innkeepers copying the Gospels, that is strange enough to elicit some comment. Ordinary people never trouble themselves with such things."

"No one asked questions about it."

"I suppose it would be best if we do not discuss this matter any further."

"Yes. I suppose not. You'll leave it lie, then?"

Stephen did not answer that. He knelt beneath the window and examined the ground. Grass and weeds grew thickly against the walls and in the places where people and horses did not go, for no sheep were let loose here as they were in the outer bailey to keep the grass under control. He was not sure what he was looking for, since after two or three days it was unlikely he would find anything useful.

"Do you see anything?" Gilbert asked.

Stephen smoothed tufts of grass out of the way so he could look at the dirt. "What does that look like to you?"

There was a half-moon impression in the dirt by one of the tufts. A pit within the crescent showed where a small stone had been dislodged. A pebble lay a few inches away. Stephen picked up the stone and set in the pit. It fit perfectly.

"That could be a heel mark," Gilbert said.

"I would say it is, more likely than not." Stephen pointed to the window. "Whoever made it stood with his back to the wall, right here. Beneath that window."

"An odd place to loiter."

"That was my thought." The sill was too high to reach even with a good jump. "That's how the thief got in. The window isn't latched. If it was, the thieves levered it up. They closed the window when they left, but couldn't reset the latch."

"Someone boosted up the man who went inside," Gilbert said, following the train of Stephen's thought.

"I'd say so, wouldn't you?"

"That sounds plausible."

"But plausibility proves nothing."

"It's a start."

"Plausibility has got us in trouble before."

"No, that was impulsiveness." Still eyeing the window, Stephen said, "Let us prove its plausibility."

"What do you mean?"

Stephen grasped Gilbert's shoulders and maneuvered him against the wall. "You stand here. You shall be the man who left the footprint."

"You're not going to —" Gilbert sputtered.

"Make a step for me with your hands. Hurry up, now."

Muttering protests, Gilbert entwined his fingers. Stephen stepped upon his hands, then climbed to Gilbert's shoulders. From this vantage point he could just reach the sill. He chinned himself upon it to show that he could do so, then gasped at Gilbert, who had remained beneath him, "You may want to get out of the way!"

As Gilbert stumbled to the side, Stephen let go. The landing was hard on his bad foot and he collapsed.

When he sat up, he noticed that a woman drawing water at the well was looking at him as if he had lost his mind. A guard on the castle wall above the woman was laughing at Stephen. He said something to someone out of sight in a nearby tower, and a second guard came out to see what was so amusing.

"They had to have done so at night," Stephen said, as Gilbert helped him to his feet.

"That is obvious, given the spectacle you have made of yourself."

"Which means they are, or were, among those quartered within this very bailey." The gate to the outer bailey was closed at sundown as the town's curfew bells rang, and the two baileys were sealed off from each other. Only those of high estate were quartered in the towers of the inner bailey: earls and those closest to them.

"It cannot be possible. We cannot be the ones to make such an accusation. I like my head where it is."

"Not yet, certainly. We'll have to have good proofs. Better ones than Brother Adolphus has."

"I thought we weren't to talk about that."

"You aren't. I can say what I please."

Gilbert sighed. "I suppose we shall have to question everyone." By everyone, it was clear he meant the magnates, who would be insulted at the suggestion of complicity.

"I'll not force that on you. We'll start with the guard and then move on to the servants. Perhaps one of them saw something."

"That doesn't seem likely if no one saw or heard what happened to poor Ormyn."

"Well, we must try something."

Chapter 6

Interviewing the guards of the inner bailey and the Prince's staff, the constable, and the earls lodged there took the remainder of the day. Stephen and Gilbert split up so that no one would go unquestioned, and they could get the business done as quickly as possible. It was grueling, asking the same questions over and over, and getting the same answers, and Stephen was exhausted by the time he and Gilbert met at the gate to the outer bailey.

"Nothing?" Stephen asked at Gilbert's resigned expression.

"Except for a messenger from Winchester arriving to much disturbance on Thursday night. People came out with torches when he arrived, apparently, but no one saw or heard anything untoward. And you?"

"The same."

"I could use a pot of ale. Not to mention something to eat."

"I like that idea." They had missed dinner in their determination to interview everyone they could as quickly as possible. There was always a lot of coming and going in the Prince's court and among the households of the earls, and they didn't want anyone who might have seen something to get away.

Gilbert frowned. "If we go back home now, Edith is likely to find something for me to do."

Gilbert was certainly right about that. There were still about two hours left in the day, and Edith abhorred wasting time when she had chores to be done, which was just about always.

"The Wobbly Kettle, then?" Stephen suggested. "That's a good place to hide."

"Hide? Who's talking about hiding? We shall be consulting about our work."

"That's what I will say if she asks what kept us."

"Good lad. You are learning. I shall have you perfectly trained up for a wife one day."

Stephen did not answer that as they turned through the main gate and headed up High Street. In his current state, he wasn't much of a prize. Women of his class selected husbands — or more accurately their parents selected on their behalf — for the groom's position and property, and he had neither. He was a cripple without anything to his name but some armor, a couple of swords, and three horses. The prospect of marriage was unlikely.

Stephen had already shared with Gilbert most of what he had seen in the chapel storage room — except for a small thing that had slipped his mind. Only as they passed Leofwine Wattepas' house at the corner of High and Mill Streets, with its fine view of both the castle and the church, did the thing come to mind. He stopped and dug around in his pouch. The little round thing was so small that he had to take everything out before he found it. He rested it in his palm and asked, "What do you make of this?"

"What is it?"

"I have no idea."

"Where did you find it?"

"In the relic's box beneath a fold of velvet."

"I cannot imagine why it would be there. Is it gold?"

"I think so. It could be bronze, though. I'm not sure."

Gilbert glanced at Wattepas' house. "Why don't we ask him? He's a goldsmith. He should know what it is."

They crossed the street to the Wattepas house, which occupied half the frontage of the block facing High Street. The shutters were still down and two journeymen, one of them Wace Bursecot, and an apprentice were working together shaping a silver bowl that could have sat comfortably on a man's head. Wace noticed them and came to the window. "Can I help you, sir?"

"Is your master about?" Stephen asked.

"Regrettably he is not."

"Perhaps then you can tell me what this is." Stephen put the little round thing on the shutter top, which served as a counter.

Wace stared at the little ring, a finger poised over it as if to prod it, but the finger hesitated and did not carry through with the gesture. Wace rubbed his lips. It was some time before he spoke, and when he did so his voice was hoarse. "Where did you get this, sir?"

"I found it in the box which had contained the relic of Saint Milburga. It's been stolen. I know you heard. I saw you at the chapel just this morning."

"News that grave is hard to keep a secret," Wace said. "We had the object in the shop only a few days ago. This," he indicated the little bit of metal, "secures the spike of a pin."

"What sort of pin would that be?"

"We attached emeralds to the relic, or relics, I should say, because the bone was in two pieces."

"How does that work?"

"A moment." Wace retreated into the back of the shop. He returned with a small pin and another little round disk with a hole in the center. He pressed the disk onto the spike of the pin. He rested the assembly in Stephen's hand. "Like that."

Stephen tried to work the disk loose. It came off, but not easily. He returned the disk and pin to Wace. "That disk, it's your work?"

"Andrew over there," Wace pointed to one of the others working on the silver bowl. "He makes them. He's better at the small stuff than the rest of us, the master excepted, of course."

"I take that as a yes."

"Of course, sir."

"How long ago was this, exactly?"

"Let me think. Four days ago. Earl Percival's steward came by with a crowd of monks to have the final work done."

"Why the steward?"

"The earl commissioned the elaboration of the relic. The monks were none too happy about it, I have to say. They moped about while we did the work, muttering and complaining."

"I should say they would!" Gilbert exclaimed. "It is outrageous. It's heresy to deface a sacred object in such a way!"

"I wonder what the point of it was?" Stephen mused.

"The earl intended to give the relic as a gift to Prince Edward," Wace said. "The steward mentioned it several times. He was quite emphatic that the settings be of the highest quality."

"Gold?"

"Naturally. But the stones themselves were the centerpiece and they were worth a fortune. Imported from Austria."

"I don't think I've ever seen an emerald."

"These were quite large." Wace extended a thumb. "Quite as large as my thumbnail, and well cut and polished, green and so luminous they seemed to shine with their own light. Beautiful objects, not a flaw in any of them. I've never seen the like and I probably never will again. A magnificent gift for the Prince." He stammered and said in a voice that seemed too loud: "Too bad they're lost now. All that work wasted."

"How many were there altogether?"

"Four, two for each fragment of bone."

Stephen nodded. He prodded the disk he had found. "Do you have a scrap of cloth? Something to wrap this in so it doesn't get lost?"

"Certainly. Just a moment." Wace retreated into the rear of the shop, and returned with a scrap of linen. He handed it to Stephen.

"You say the earl planned to make a gift of the emeralds to the Prince," Stephen said.

"Yes," Wace said.

"After they were fixed to the relic."

"So the steward said."

"Which means that the earl planned to give the relic also."

"That seemed plain."

"I cannot believe that."

"It is what I heard."

Stephen was shocked at the suggestion that FitzAllen could give away something belonging to the priory. He glanced at Gilbert, whom he was sure would be equally shocked. But he saw only a long face and a drooping mouth, with Gilbert's hands stroking his cheeks.

"Is that all?" Wace asked. "It is late and we still have work to do before we are allowed our supper."

"Thank you, yes."

Wace pulled up the shutters so he did not have to respond to any afterthoughts from Stephen.

As Stephen stepped toward Broad Street with Gilbert moping at his side, he asked, "How is the earl able to give away the relic?"

"Because it belongs to him," Gilbert said. "The priory is merely its repository."

"How did that come to be?"

"The relic was found in the graveyard of the village church, more than a hundred-fifty years ago. The land belonged to the Wybern family, who held the manor at that time. They deposited it with the priority, but did not make it a gift. Ownership came to the FitzAllens through their marriage to the one of the Wybern heiresses. Most people have forgotten this, but the monks of Greater Wenlock have not and apparently neither has FitzAllen."

"FitzAllen does not hold the manor?"

"No, his father sold it to pay off some debt or other. His connection with Greater Wenlock is thin. I'm surprised he even knew about the relic, to tell you the truth."

They turned onto Broad Street where John le Spicer kept his shop on the corner. John the elder was in the doorway just closing up, and they exchanged greetings. He had started as an apothecary, but his son had gone into the wine business. The location was perfect for the wine trade, since it enabled sales to be made to anyone passing down High and Broad Streets or coming to the market. They had recently torn down and rebuilt the house so that it was almost as grand as the Wattepas mansion.

Stephen and Gilbert began the steep descent down Broad Street, watchful for piles of horse and dog manure — and the occasional spills of human offal — which plagued the streets despite the efforts of the town bailiffs to require those with houses along the way to keep their doorsteps clean. When Stephen had first come to Ludlow briefly as a boy to squire at the castle before his father had sent him to London to read the law, he had given no thought to the town. When he had returned last autumn, at first he had regarded it as a place of exile, but he had grown to look upon it with some affection. The panorama down Broad Street was one of those that warmed him as much as the view from his garret window, with the houses on either side of the street marching downhill in solid walls, neat and tidy and prosperous, the street curving gently right, concluding at the gate tower at the bottom, and beyond the rising hills on the opposite bank of the River Teme covered with trees.

"That's odd," he said when they were halfway to the gate and just passing Bell Lane.

"What's odd?"

"I don't see Harry." Harry's licensed begging spot was just inside the gate. He was visible from Bell Lane when he was occupying it. It was early for Harry to have abandoned his post, and that was the source of some concern. It was unlike Harry to give up the chance to collect a farthing.

"Perhaps it was the prospect of rain," Gilbert said, for although the day had begun with a clear sky, an overcast had rolled in, low, dark, and threatening. "You know how he hates to get wet."

"I know he complains about it, but when have you known him to run from a few raindrops?"

"You have me there."

When they reached the gate, Stephen called to Gip, the toothless gate ward who was sheltering in his niche, "What happened to Harry?"

"He's gone to the Kettle," Gip called back. "Getting airs that one. Thinks he's better than ordinary people now. And we've you to thank for it."

"I bear no responsibility for anything Harry does."

"Well, you're the one who forced him to take a bath last month. Now he thinks he's got to have one regular. He said I could use one myself, that he could smell me all the way out in the street. The cheek! If he wasn't so short, I'd smack him in the head, but it's too much trouble to lean over."

"Good God!" Gilbert said as they passed on to Lower Broad Street, where the Wobbly Kettle sat just before the bridge. "Harry bathing once a month? I can't believe it."

"The foundations of the earth are trembling," Stephen said.

The Wobbly Kettle lay just over a hundred yards ahead beside a water mill at the foot of the bridge. The prior of Saint John's Hospital across the street stood on his doorstep and glared as they went inside to convey his disapproval of their visit to the bawdy house, but he said nothing. The town whores needed somewhere to ply their trade, and the town elders did not want them on the streets where they might bother men walking about with their wives and families.

The front room was stuffy from the fire burning in the fireplace, one of the few in town because they were so expensive to build. The room was otherwise unoccupied except for a pair of whores lounging on a bench, but it was early yet. Harry's platform leaned against the wall behind the door. Stephen bought mugs of ale for himself and Gilbert, and they pushed into the rear, where the tubs for bathing were kept in a long shed that stretched behind the house, each tub separated by curtains.

Stephen peeked through the gaps in the curtains until he found Harry in the third tub on the left. A girl was also there, holding a comb, scissors, and razor.

"Damn it," Harry said as Stephen and Gilbert entered and sat on the bench beside the tub. "Can't a man bathe in peace without being bothered by the likes of you?"

"We were so amazed when we heard you'd come here of your own choice that we rushed immediately to verify the rumor," Stephen said.

"No one would believe it without proof," Gilbert said.

"Well, you've seen it," Harry said. "Now off with you. Unless you'd care to share some of that ale. Hot water is damnably expensive. So I've used up all my money."

"Water does cost money," Stephen said.

"Actually, I think it's the wood," Gilbert said.

"Someone has to carry water from the river," Stephen said. "I doubt they do it for free."

"Are you going to waste my valuable time with idle chit chat or are you going to share that ale?" Harry demanded.

"You are making yourself unpleasant," Stephen said. But he handed Harry his mug.

Gilbert was heard to murmur, "He is always unpleasant." At Harry's glare, Gilbert regarded the ceiling, twiddling his thumbs on his ample stomach as if he had not spoken.

The girl asked rather impatiently, "Do you want a shave or not?"

"A moment, dear," Harry said. "I'm thinking. This is an important decision, and I am torn. And they have interrupted my thoughts. Give me time to collect myself."

"There is so little of you left that it should not take long," Gilbert muttered.

"You look better without the beard," she said. One might doubt she meant this sincerely, since she stood to gain if he yielded. But it had turned out that under what had been a terrible mat of beard, Harry in fact was a handsome man, a matter which had not gone unnoticed in the town.

"That is the problem," Harry said. "With the beard I am more pitiful and attract more charity. Without it, I only attract women." Harry pointed at Stephen. "And it's his fault I am in this conundrum. He forced a shave upon me, and it's nearly ruined me. Every time I turn around some girl wants to take me home. But there's no profit in that."

The girl ruffled Harry's hair. "Poor baby. I bet they wish they had that problem."

"Why don't you compromise," Stephen said. "Make it a short trim."

"I had not thought of that," Harry said. "It might do. All right. Let's do that."

He raised his bearded chin and the girl set down the razor and went to work with the comb and scissors. In short order, she trimmed the beard close but left a rakish point at the chin. Stephen had to admit that the effect was excellent.

"Would you mind paying Emily?" Harry asked.

"I paid once already," Stephen said. "This one is on you."

"I know. With that." Harry indicated a block of wood lying on the bench beside Stephen, who had paid no attention to it when he sat down.

Stephen picked up the block. He saw that one end was carved. It was a woman's face. As he held it up, it became clear that it was Emily's face.

"That is a good likeness," Stephen said, amazed as he held it out to Emily.

She took it, planted a kiss on Harry's head, and left them. They heard her calling to someone beyond the curtains to show them her likeness, and there was a babble as several women gathered to admire it.

Stephen retrieved a clay pot sitting beside the barrel. It still held some ale, and he replenished their cups. He poked his head out of the curtains and called for a refill. One of the women clustered about Emily accepted the pitcher. Stephen sat back down on the bench.

"I trust my messengers found you this morning," Harry said.

"You sent the boys?"

"They were loitering about my spot discussing their find."

"Yes, they found me." Stephen briefly recounted the finding of Ormyn's body and his examination.

"Naked, you said," Harry said, taking another sip. "The Thumpers will have the whys and wherefores of that."

"That's what we thought," Stephen said.

"What did they have to say about it?"

"I haven't talked to them yet."

"What! Why not?"

"Something else has come up. Something deemed more important."

"What could be more important than murder?"

"You haven't heard, then?"

"You wouldn't be talking about that bunch of bones."

"Not a bunch of bones," Gilbert said. "A sacred relic of Saint Milburga. It's one bone, actually, a piece of the thigh broken in two."

"What do you have to do with that?" Harry asked.

"We're to find it," Gilbert said.

"Why would anyone want to steal the relic?" Harry asked. "You can't sell something like that."

"Why, to have it, of course."

"Who would want just to have it?"

"Another religious house perhaps," Gilbert speculated. "The competition for relics can get quite fierce, I am afraid to say."

"Another house might buy it? That hardly seems likely. They'd not be able to tell anyone they had it. Word would get out and FitzAllen would demand its return. Good God, he might even summon lawyers. No one wants to have them involved."

"Perhaps some rich man who feels in need of the protection the relic provides," Stephen said.

"I'd not take such a risk or incur such an expense," Harry said.

"What if you were dying, or someone close to you was dying? You might then."

"But if that was the case, he could simply pay the monks for a view of it, and make a prayer. Much easier than theft."

Harry pursed his lips. "I heard that it was encrusted with jewels."

"I don't think encrusted quite describes it," Stephen said. "There were four jewels attached, two on each fragment. That hardly counts as encrusted."

"Emeralds," Gilbert said, his disapproval plain.

"Ah, emeralds," Harry said, as if he had a deep knowledge of emeralds, although he had no idea what one looked like.

"Yes, FitzAllen recently had them put on," Stephen said. "By Wattepas. He intended to give the relic to the Prince. The gems were to enhance the gift, to make it more precious."

"He can do that?" Harry asked.

"Do what?" Stephen replied.

"Give away someone's relic."

"It was his."

"That's hard to believe."

"Nonetheless," Gilbert said, "it is true."

"Well, you were at Greater Wenlock. You should know."

"Indeed, I was," Gilbert said with obvious regret.

"You knew this?" Stephen asked.

"Of course, I knew it," Harry said. "He mopes about it, especially when he's drunk. You haven't heard him? He stole that Gospel of his when he ran off with Edith, too."

"So I've learned."

"I did not steal it," Gilbert said. "It was mine."

"Fat chance of that." Harry sat up. "He looks honest but behind that cheery face lurks a heart filled with avarice and lust. Don't be fooled."

"Stop it," Gilbert said.

"Let's talk about something else," Stephen said in an effort to change the subject.

Fortunately for Stephen's effort, the girl who had fetched away the pitcher returned with it. Gilbert refilled their mugs. Stephen was beginning to feel a little lightheaded from the ale, even though it was weak. He worried that Harry might also be feeling its effects since he had been drinking longer. Stephen had never seen a drunk Harry, and the prospect was frightening. Harry was bad enough when he was sober. But Harry's cup was recharged before he could say anything about it.

"Have you given any thought to the possibility that your thief was after the jewels, and not the relic itself?" Harry asked.

Stephen kept his mouth from falling open with a conscious effort. This had not occurred to him. He had simply assumed that the relic was the object of the theft. This could be, he reflected during the fleeting moment available, another of his mistakes. He had leapt to conclusions before, and they had led him astray.

"Of course we thought of that," Stephen said. "Didn't we, Gilbert?"

"Yes, naturally," Gilbert said without any hesitation. "But the relic is the more precious object that a few baubles. It had to be the relic the thief was after."

"Hmmph," Harry snorted. "If it was me, I'd be after those stones. They're probably worth a lot, and much easier to sell, if your thief has a mind to do that."

"Well," Stephen said, "they are certainly worth quite a lot by themselves, that's true."

"You have a criminal mind," Gilbert said.

"It's not my mind that's criminal," Harry said, "I just understand them better than you, you pious wretch."

"Well, thank you for the pious part, anyway."

"Yer welcome." Harry's fingers flicked the surface of the water in the tub. "It's getting cold. I think I'm done. Would you call for the porter?"

"What," Gilbert said, "having trouble getting out yourself?"

"I've already paid for them to remove me. More dignified that way. I must keep up appearances, you know."

"Appearances are important," Stephen said, rising and heading for the gap in the curtains.

"Quite so. Gilbert, good fellow, you wouldn't mind arranging my raiments so I can get at them handily, would you?"

The porters not only lifted Harry from the tub, but they helped dry him off and dress him, and then they carried him up the steps into the house and deposited him in the front hall by his board.

Stephen opened the door but hesitated to step outside. It had begun to rain, not a heavy downpour, but a steady one. The street was already sodden, with a stream coursing down the center, and it would not take much churning to turn it into Ludlow's famous mud.

"You wouldn't mind lending us a couple of cloaks?" Stephen asked Ted, the proprietor, who was wiping up a spill on one of the tables. "We've neglected to bring ours."

"Lending?" Ted asked, as if the thought of giving value without getting any in return was a foreign idea. "I suppose I could." He spoke to one of the girls, and she went out, returning shortly with two cloaks, one for Stephen and one for Gilbert.

"None for me?" Harry asked.

"If I give you one, I've no assurance I'll ever see it again," Ted said, "You'd likely sell it first thing." He flung his towel over a shoulder and left the hall.

The three went outside, but lingered in the shelter afforded by the overhanging upper stories of the house before plunging into the wet.

"Damn it," Harry said. "All that money spent on getting clean wasted."

Stephen looked down on Harry, strapped to his board and glowering in dismay at the prospect of the long haul up the hill to Bell Lane. There was no one on the street owing to the rain, and Saint John's Hospital's shutters were closed and the prior nowhere in view. Feeling a bit drunk and wobbly, Stephen passed his borrowed cloak to Gilbert.

He squatted down to bring his head level with Harry's. "I'll carry you, but if you say anything about it to anyone, I'll have your tongue out."

"Tongue out. Got it."

Harry unstrapped himself as Stephen turned his back. Harry put an arm around Stephen's neck. Stephen stood up. It took a great deal of effort, since Harry was solid and heavy, but he managed it without staggering.

"For God's sake, man," Stephen sputtered. "Go easy! You're choking me."

"Sorry." Harry lowered his arm, which was as thick and sturdy as an oak limb, from Stephen's neck.

"I'll take that cloak now," Stephen said to Gilbert, who draped the cloak over the both of them. "Pull the hood down so no one sees who I am."

"This isn't going to fool anyone," Gilbert said.

"If we go quickly, no one will see. Don't forget Harry's board."

Stephen stepped into the wet, walking carefully so as not to slip in the mud.

"You look like a hunchback," Gilbert said as he caught up.

"I like that," Harry said, his breath on the back of Stephen's neck. "The hunchback of Ludlow. It rolls off the tongue better than the gimp of Ludlow."

"Oh, shut up," Stephen said, and he plodded up the hill to Broad Gate.

Chapter 7

The problem of Ormyn's death was on Stephen's mind when he awoke the next morning. He had nothing to gain by spending time contemplating the matter, even if there was a chance of finding the answer, which there was not. No one had seen or heard a thing, not a cry for help or for fear, or the crashing of Ormyn's body into the hazel wood on the slope. Yet all he could think of as he lay in bed were imaginings of Ormyn's last moments — the confrontation with the killers, what might have been said to lull him into suspecting nothing, how they lifted him above the parapet, Ormyn's terror and his sense of helplessness in those final moments, and the long fall into the eternal night. Perhaps it was the funeral that brought these thoughts to his attention. It was to be held later in the morning after Prime. He didn't want to go, but he had to.

When it became clear that the sun was going to insist on rising, Stephen threw aside the blanket and stumbled to the table before the window. He swabbed his face, arms, and chest with a wet cloth from the basin. He opened the shutters and wrung out the cloth, which he lay on the windowsill to dry, and stuck his head out to check below for pedestrians before he dumped the contents of the basin.

He heard voices in the yard, which was still in shadow, for the sun had not climbed more than half a fist's width from the horizon. Stephen saw Jennifer Wistwode, Gilbert's daughter, sitting on a bench at the stable with Harry at her feet. She resembled her parents too closely for anyone to call Jennie pretty, a stout girl with a round, blunt face, but she was lively and happy, and so she did not lack for admirers. The fact that lately she had such stolen moments with Harry was a cause of worry to her parents, since anyone spending too much time in Harry's company was likely to be corrupted beyond salvation. It was a Sunday, and begging wasn't allowed on Sundays, so Harry had the day off. He said something that Stephen did not catch which made Jennifer laugh. She leaned over and tugged the new point of Harry's beard. Harry's blush was so intense that Stephen could see it even at this distance in the bad light.

Then Edith's voice could be heard calling Jennifer to get ready for Sunday Mass. Jennifer shot to her feet and hurried across the yard. Harry watched her go with a wistful expression until he became aware that Stephen was watching from above.

"Careful there," Harry called, "I'm not catching you when you fall out."

"Come on over, I'll give you another bath." Stephen held out the basin.

"Not today, thanks."

As Stephen finished pouring the basin water into the yard, the Wistwode family emerged — Gilbert, Edith, Jennie, Gilbert the younger, and baby Howard who was not yet a year old in the arms of his nurse. Edith spotted Stephen before he could duck out of sight.

She shook a finger at him. "Why are you not ready?"

"I think I'll pass," Stephen said, peering around the window frame, embarrassed that he was half naked and that she had probably seen it. "Perhaps this afternoon."

"You're not thinking of making him go to Mass?" Harry asked. "Remember what happened the last time, dead bodies everywhere in the churchyard."

"There were not dead bodies everywhere," Edith retorted. "There was only the one, that poor girl frozen under the path."

"Yes, well, you're sure to find another. There are bodies lying about wherever Stephen goes."

"I've had enough of you this morning, Harry. Find something useful to do if you too are unwilling to attend Mass." Edith turned about. "Gilbert! Let us leave these two to their fate."

"I have something useful to do," Harry mouthed to Edith's back. While Harry's tongue could cut others like a sword, he was careful around Edith.

Now that Edith was out of the house and he was safe, Stephen went down to the hall. He collected a new loaf of bread, still warm and soft, and a half roll of cheese, and went out to the stable. Jennie should already have delivered Harry's breakfast, but since Harry was always hungry, Stephen broke the loaf and the cheese in half and left those pieces on the bench for him.

"What are you working on?" Stephen asked. "Another of the bath-house girls?"

Harry had bent to another block of wood on which he was carving. "No."

Harry did not offer any further explanation, so Stephen pressed on. "Who then?"

"Nobody." Harry reached for the bread and cheese.

Stephen moved them away. "Nothing until you show me."

"You are a swine."

"No, I am trying to show polite interest. You are the swine."

Harry regarded the bread and cheese, as if considering an attempt to snatch them from Stephen's hand. "All right, then," he said, surrendering the block of wood.

It was not one of the bath-house girls after all, but a likeness of the girl Rosamond whom Harry, and in fact not Stephen, had found dead in the churchyard last Christmas Day.

"This is good," Stephen said, giving back the carving. "You should show it to the prior at Saint Laurence's."

"Why?"

"He might be interested in acquiring it."

"He'll want me to make a gift of it. Besides, Jennie wants it."

"What should she want with a likeness of Rosamond?"

"She thinks it will bring good luck."

"Whatever gave her the idea it would do that?"

Harry shrugged. "I don't know. People think funny things."

"This isn't the first such carving you've made of her."

"I might have done one or two more."

"One or two more!"

"I gave her one before, my first one, in fact. She gave it away to someone else. Now she needs another."

"And this other one or two? What happened to them?"

"They might've got sold."

"Does Gilbert know you're dealing in Rosamond's likeness?"

"No, and don't you tell him. He might be inspired to raise my rent, or something." Harry lived in one of the stalls used for storing hay.

"I cannot believe that you're profiting from that poor girl's death."

"If it wasn't me, it'd be somebody else. Besides, I've got to do something to make up for what I've lost in begging. People aren't as charitable after what you did to me."

"Don't blame me. Now you've gone and done it to yourself."

Harry stroked his trimmed beard and grinned. "Jennie likes me beard this way."

"It is an improvement."

"So, Gilbert said that you asked Sir Geoff yesterday to take you on as a knight."

Stephen did not say anything.

"And he refused. Owing to your disability."

Stephen nodded.

"You know, I've told you time and again to sell that damned horse, since you've got no real need for him. You could make a fortune, maybe even enough to buy a small plot of land, set yourself up as a gentleman. They say a horse like that is worth a lot."

"He is."

"Well, then, see some sense. If you can't be a soldier, you can at least amuse yourself lording it over your tenants."

"I'll not sell the horse." This sort of talk almost always put Stephen in a sulk, especially since there was some truth in what Harry said: he might get enough from the sale of the horse to buy a small manor. Rich merchants bought manors all the time and thereby entered the gentry. Yet he could not bring himself to take this step. He could not put words to why. It just felt like going down rather than up, and he was too far down already.

Seeing that Stephen would not be moved by this old argument, Harry changed subjects. "How does that work, exactly?"

"What do you mean?"

"Well, I've seen you don't use the stirrup on the left side. What's keeping you?"

Stephen thought about explaining it, but Harry could not ride a horse and words might not paint a clear picture. There was no one in view, so he went into the stable and removed one of the stirrup leathers from his saddle. He sat back on the bench and removed his boot and sock so that Harry could see his stump. He dangled the stirrup and put the remains of his foot onto it. "Look here. You can see there is hardly enough left to get a purchase on the stirrup."

"But you're managing."

"Only because we're sitting still. But there's a grave risk that my foot will slip through, like this." Stephen pushed the heel through the stirrup so that the stirrup hung on his ankle. "This is bad, and if I happen to fall, the horse can drag me to my death."

"That would be unpleasant."

Stephen pulled his foot back through the stirrup. "In battle, you have to be able to stand securely in the stirrups as you wield a sword. The danger of slipping through then is magnified. Falls are common."

"So Sir Geoff wouldn't take you on because of that?"

"That's his story."

"You poor dear. Life is full of disappointments. You'll just have to get used to your little measure."

"Yes, it is, isn't it?" Stephen lay the stirrup on the ground and put his sock and boot back on before anyone stuck his head out of the house, not that anyone really cared what they were doing out here.

Harry picked up the stirrup. "There might be something I can do with this."

"What are you talking about?"

"Just leave it with me for a few days. I've an idea."

"What if I am called to journey somewhere? I've this relic to find. I doubt it's anywhere close by now."

"You don't need the stirrup. You don't use it."

Stephen sighed. "Well, that's true. It's no better than a decoration."

The climb up the hill from Bell Lane could leave even a fit person panting, and Stephen was breathing hard by the time he reached the wine shop at the corner, where a disturbance had broken out. Almost a dozen rough-looking men who had to be soldiers were clustered about the shop, banging on the shutters and demanding that the Spicers open up.

A voice within the shop shouted that it was Sunday, and the shop dared not open, to which one of the men outside shouted back, "Fuck Sunday! We want drink!"

"Well, you can't have it!" the voice within the shop answered, although the waver in the tone did not sound convincing.

"You know, boys," Stephen said to their backs, "the town bailiffs are just over there." He gestured toward the Guild Hall which stood halfway down High Street.

"Piss off," said a fellow with a great black moustache.

"I don't see no fucking bailiffs," said another, whose sagging jowls and squinting eyes made him resemble a bulldog.

"You want trouble?" asked a third.

"Just trying to give you some friendly advice," Stephen said. He could practically smell the menace. It wouldn't take much for this crowd to turn on him if Spicer didn't open his shop and they didn't get what they wanted.

"You can stick your advice up your ass," came the reply as the pounding redoubled. The racket was loud enough that faces began appearing in the windows along Broad Street, but no one dared come out to intervene. The number of assaults and affrays had mushroomed since the town had swelled with soldiers, and most of the victims were townspeople. Pleas to the castle had brought declarations from the officers that they would bring things under control, but the locals had not detected any changes yet.

John the Younger at last lost his nerve and dropped one of the shutters. He backed away and one of his boys appeared in his place, hastily placing clay cups on the shutter, which served as a counter. He started to fill the cups from a pitcher, but he spilled so much and was so slow that one of the soldiers took the pitcher from his hand and did the job for him.

"Give us another!" one of the soldiers cried, referring to the pitcher, which had emptied immediately.

The boy produced a replacement, which was promptly swept off the counter and passed among the soldiers, many of whom did not bother with a cup but drank directly from the pitcher.

"Sirs! Sirs! The charge!" John the Younger called from a prudent distance within the shop where he was out of reach in case the soldiers took offense at the request for payment.

One of the men tossed a few coins through the open window. The rest of the men ignored the plea. It must have been enough because John the Younger did not protest any further. But perhaps he was happy to be paid at all. There had been a problem with payment at other establishments.

"What're you looking at?" one of the soldiers asked Stephen, lowering the pitcher from his mouth, wine soaking his beard and dripping on his coat.

Stephen regretted that he had said anything. He'd had the vague notion that he should do something about such open and obvious lawbreaking, but exactly what, since he was alone, was unclear. It was easy from one's armchair to suggest that he should put a stop to this open law-breaking, but another when you were alone before ten hard men eager for their pleasure.

The soldiers looked more closely at Stephen. Although some of them might enjoy a good beating now that they were fueled with wine, they hesitated, for the quality of Stephen's blue coat and red-green stockings, though patched in places and fraying in others, said that he was a member of the minor gentry. The fellows' senses had not dulled so much yet that they did not consider to whom Stephen might be connected and the cost to themselves of a bit of rough fun at his expense.

"Who are you?" one of the soldiers asked.

"My name is Stephen Attebrook. I am the deputy coroner here."

"Look at you," said a soldier as he took up the pitcher. "Must not pay much."

This brought a laugh.

"You're right about that," Stephen said. "But the fact remains, as a crown officer, one of my responsibilities is to keep the peace. Which means I'll have to report you to the castle if you don't cease and desist now."

"Go ahead," the soldier with the pitcher said. He put it on the counter and beckoned for a refill. "Won't do no good. Our lord, he don't care if we have a bit of fun."

"No one objects to you having fun. This is not the time or place for it."

Stephen expected another sharp retort, but the eyes of the men went to something behind him. Stephen heard a horse approaching. He half turned to keep the mob in view while he looked at whoever was coming.

There were two horses rather than one. The riders stopped their mounts. The leader was well dressed in a green outer tunic; its sleeves were unbuttoned and the man's arms were out of them. His under tunic was blue and red with silver buttons at the cuff. He wore high boots which looked to be new, with hardly a crease on them.

"Sergeant," the leader said, "I want the wagons loaded as soon as possible. There's lots of work to do and no time to waste."

"You heard him," the sergeant said to the soldiers. Those who had cups put them on the counter and the group straggled toward the castle. A pitcher was left lying in the street. Stephen retrieved it and set it on the counter.

"I trust they weren't too much trouble," the lord said to Stephen, although his tone indicated that he knew they had been.

"Not out of the ordinary," Stephen said.

The lord chuckled. "I should know better than to pay men on a Sunday. You're Randall's man, aren't you?"

"That's right."

"I'm Richard Parfet." He leaned over and extended his hand.

Stephen shook it. "Stephen Attebrook."

"I'd stop and chat, but as I said, we've work to do. Melmerby," Parfet addressed the dark-haired and mustachioed fellow beside him festooned with canteens and drinking skins, "have those filled, and no drinking yourself. I don't want you falling off your horse. You always do that when you're drunk."

"No need to worry about me, sir," Melmerby said.

"I always have to worry about you, Melmerby."

"Good day," Parfet said to Stephen and turned his horse toward the castle.

Melmerby got off his horse, but in doing so, he dropped an armload of wineskins and canteens. He looked up at Stephen almost as if he expected some help in recovering them. But he knew better than to expect this from Stephen, and scrabbled after the fallen canteens without any assistance.

Thoughts of the Thumpers had come back to mind now that the crisis at the wine shop had passed. It was early yet for the funeral, so Stephen left Melmerby to scramble in the dirt for the canteens as he turned east on High Street and strode for Galdeford Gate.

A bun seller whose shop stood just within the gate waved to him from her open door. He was surprised to see her, since businesses in the town were not allowed to be open on Sunday, when everyone was expected to attend Mass. But as at the wine shop, things were not as they should be, owing to the presence of the army. He knew he should just walk by. But temptation got the better of him.

"Clara, there wouldn't be a bun just inside the door?" he asked.

"There might be," Clara said, ducking inside and beckoning him to follow.

There was indeed a tray of buns. Stephen sniffed the air. No smell of fresh baking, unfortunately. "Left-overs, eh?" he asked.

"You'd think with all the soldiers in town, business would be better, but they fancy ale and women more than they do a good bun."

"Savages, that's what they are. How old are they?"

"Baked yesterday."

"I'll take two, no, three. Could you put a little extra honey on them?"

"Only for you, dear." Clara disappeared into the back of the house, where several children could be heard in a dispute over a game of hoops. She returned with a small clay bottle. She unstoppered the bottle and dribbled honey on the three buns Stephen had selected. She put a finger to her lips. "No telling the bailiffs, now."

"It's just a gift, for a toiling public servant," Stephen said.

"Of course it is. Oh! Look what you've dropped!" Clara collected the fragment of a pence Stephen had left on the tray.

"I don't see anything," Stephen said, mouth so full of bun that his words were barely understandable.

"It's a pity about that Ormyn fellow. Did you know him?"

Stephen nodded. He knew all the castle guards at least by sight, since he trained sword-and-shield fighting with them most mornings.

"I wonder what will happen to the children," Clara said.

"What do you mean?"

"There'll be no one to look after them now."

"Why? There's a widow. Surely she'll make provision."

"They're *step*-children," Clara said. "Bridget can't be counted on to take care of them, and Ormyn had no other family, that I know of."

"You are remarkably well informed." Stephen wished he had paid more attention, but then he rarely lingered after practice, and, anyway, men seldom spoke of their families; it was a subject out of bounds, and one never probed about it.

Clara sniffed. "It's a small town, and I keep my ears open. As I'd expect of you too, given your business." She gestured toward the gate. "Why, it wasn't but last year that Bridget turned up. A pretty young thing, fourteen if a day. Spoiled not at all yet by hard living. She took up at first with some of that riff-raff that lived in the town ditch. Begged at the bridge there, much to One-Eye Dick's ire. It was on the Galdeford side so the wardens couldn't do anything about her, owing as she never bothered to get a town license. She almost got into a fight with Dick, came to knives drawn. But nobody did anything about that, either."

"She was a beggar at the bridge?" Stephen asked, astonished.

"That's what I just said. Not for long, though. She got a job at the Crow and then at the Pigeon. She's got ambitions, that one, I'll warrant." The Crow was a tavern in Upper Galdeford not far away, and the Pigeon was a better class of inn on Corve Street north of town by the River Corve bridge.

"Sounds like a girl down on her luck willing to work hard."

"Work hard on her back, I'd say. I'll bet if you asked Herb at the Pigeon you'll find she turned a trick or two upstairs."

"Except I don't see the reason to ask. What Bridget has done in her past life is not my concern."

The bun seller laughed. "But it do make interesting conversation, eh?"

"On a dull Sunday, I suppose. If this was a dull Sunday, which it isn't. I must be going. I've lots to do."

"Enjoy your bun, dear."

"I always do."

Stephen took his leave, and passed through the gate. A section of the bridge over the ditch was roped off where it had burned late in the winter. Paupers often took refuge under the town bridges in bad weather, and one such party's fire had caught the timbers of the bridge and burned a hole through the top before the fire watch had managed to extinguish it. It should have been repaired already, but the city fathers were debating whether to apply a patch or replace the structure entirely. Both cost money, and at the moment, money was in short supply. There was a great deal of opposition to adding a special tax to cover the expense because so many people were stretched from meeting the high price of corn, which had been driven up by the Welsh war and the coming of the English army.

A short distance beyond the gate the road forked, the left going to Upper Galdeford and the right to Lower Galdeford. Stephen went right. As he passed the stone cross at the fork, he remembered another time he had come this way, and the owl that had sat upon the stone cross. A fat raven occupied the cross now. It paused in poking the feathers under one wing to watch Stephen pass, cocking its head as if to get a good view of the surviving bun in Stephen's hand.

"You can't have it," Stephen said, stuffing the bun into his mouth and licking the honey from his fingers.

The houses along Lower Galdeford Street dribbled out to pastures and fields after a hundred yards or so, and it wasn't long before he reached the orchard surrounding the Augustine priory that lay to the east of town. The scaffolding was still up on the church tower, but no one was working on it, as it was Sunday.

Beyond the priory, he came to a footpath leading toward the river. A wicker fence ran along the path and on the other side was a huge dung pile towering over a shack. The last time Stephen had come here, in search of a valuable list of the supporters of Simon de Montfort, he had hopped the fence and crossed the yard to the house, but this time, his visit was an official one, so he kept to the road until he came to the gate. It was an old house that had been added onto several times as if at a whimsy, with the newer parts forming the upper arms of what, more or less, stood in the shape of a U.

Children playing in the yard spotted him and ran into the house to warn of his approach, so Will Thumper, a short muscular fellow with graying black hair, and half his family were already outside waiting for him. Since Thumper had an enormous family, even the half made a good crowd. They did not look welcoming.

"G'morning, Will," Stephen said with false cheer. "Nice barn you have there." It was, in fact, a brand new barn, made of fresh wood. The thatch was still yellow.

Thumper made a sour face at mention of the barn. He had Stephen to thank for the fact it was new. Stephen had set fire to the old one to cover his escape after he had broken into Thumper's house. "What do you want?"

"I want to talk to Tad."

"Tad's got nothing to say to you."

"This is official business. Bring him out, or I go to the sheriff and have him hauled out. If that happens, the deputies might be inclined to search your house. I don't think you want them to have a look inside that storeroom of yours." Thumper was a man of many enterprises. One of them included dealing in stolen property, if not outright theft. Stephen had discovered his storeroom, which held that stolen property. Stephen had exchanged silence about the storeroom for Thumper's willingness to drop his appeal about the burning of the barn.

"We've a deal on that. You're breaking it now?"

"Oh, I won't say anything. But who knows how far those boys will have to go to find Tad."

"What official business?"

"A man was found dead outside the castle. One of the guards named Ormyn. Someone tossed him off the wall. You must have heard of it. The whole town knows."

"We had nothing to do with that."

"I'm not accusing you. But Tad found the body and didn't tell anyone, except for a few of the town boys."

Thumper's mouth, already sagging at the corners, sagged even further. "He told some town boys?"

"That's why I've come to you."

Thumper spoke to an older woman whose hair was as gray as the thatch of the house, and just as disheveled. "Get Tad out here!"

The woman marched back to the house. She was gone a long time. Stephen wondered if Tad had taken to the rafters or some other hiding place when the children had announced his arrival, for he must know the purpose of Stephen's errand. If Tad had gone into hiding, he could not evade the old woman who was probably skilled in finding hiding children, for presently she returned, dragging Tad by the collar. He was bigger than Stephen remembered, twelve or thirteen, and almost as tall as a man with hair that stuck out like a hay rick. The woman flung him at Thumper, who caught him and began to administer a beating with the cudgel he always carried in his belt. Tad fell to the ground under the rain of blows and curses, curling into a ball and covering his head.

Stephen allowed a few blows to connect before he stepped in. He caught the cudgel in mid-blow and stripped it from Thumper's grasp. Then he hauled Tad to his feet. Thumper looked furious, whether at Stephen for his intervention or at Tad it was hard to say. Probably both. But since Thumper already knew that Stephen's skill with a cudgel was formidable, and since this visit was official, he did not object to being disarmed.

Stephen tossed the cudgel to Thumper and drew Tad across the yard away from the crowd to the shelter of an oak. He sat the boy on the ground at the base of the tree and stood over him. Tad had recovered quickly from the brief beating, probably because he was used to beatings, and he wore a sullen but cautious expression, eyes flicking toward his father who had followed them.

"You aren't talking to him that I don't hear," Thumper said.

"No, I will talk to Tad alone," Stephen said. He figured that Tad might be more inclined to be truthful if Thumper did not overhear. This would enable him to lie freely about what they said.

After some hesitation, Thumper retreated across the yard.

Stephen squatted by Tad. Tad squinted at him. "Those snitches," Tad said. "I'll get them."

"No, you won't. You're to leave them alone. Surely you must know that your find would be known eventually. Such things can't be kept secret. Somebody always talks. Does your father know you made them pay?"

"You know about that?"

"Of course, I know."

"He don't know."

"So you've kept the money for yourself?"

"You going to tell?"

"That bit's your affair. I want to know how you found him."

"We was playing on the hill. And there he was. Lying dead as a door-nail."

"You? Playing? Where nobody ever goes? Come on. I'm not that stupid."

Tad looked worried. "I can't. He'll have my head off, if I do."

"Your father had a hand in this? Was he there?"

"Not exactly."

"Not exactly a hand, or he was there?"

"He was there."

Stephen had not expected this answer and it took a moment for him to absorb it. "What were you up to?"

"Don't make me tell. Please!"

Whatever they had been doing it had to be seriously illegal for Tad to plead like this. Scheming and lying came naturally, but he wasn't the pleading sort.

"Did this have anything to do with the theft of Saint Milburga's bones?"

"You'll have to ask dad. I'm not saying nothing more."

Stephen stood and beckoned to Will Thumper. Thumper swaggered over. "You were there when Ormyn's body was found," Stephen said.

"He told you that?"

"An astute guess. What were you doing up there?"

"A bit of business."

"So I heard. You'll have to tell me, Will. Or I'll take young Tad up to the castle and let the boys there pry it out of him."

To Stephen's astonishment, Thumper laughed. "You do that. You just do that. Won't do no good. I'm good friends with them now."

Stephen frowned. Thumper, a friend with the castle garrison now? "I suppose I shall have to ask them how such an incredible thing is possible."

Thumper looked alarmed, realizing that he had said too much. "Look, it wasn't nothing illegal."

"That's not the impression I got. Nor the one you're giving me now."

"It wasn't illegal for us."

"Not for you? But for whom?"

"Look, if you keep quiet about it, I'll let you on to a little piece of it."

"Thumper, bribing a crown official is a serious crime."

"What? It happens all the time."

"I think we're done here." Stephen stepped toward the gate.

Thumper caught his arm. "Look, it's honest work for a change. Don't spoil it."

"Tell me what it was, and perhaps I can find a way to forebear."

Thumper rubbed his hands on his shirt. "All right, then. Every night I take a couple of my girls and a few of the neighbor girls up to the castle. There's that old sally port on the north side, beneath the northwest tower."

"I know of it."

"The sergeant of the guard comes down and unlocks the grate for us and lets us in."

"He lets you in the castle?"

"Not in the castle, exactly. Into the tunnel."

"The one that runs into the tower?"

"That's it. There's only one tunnel I know of."

"And what do you do there?" Stephen asked the question, although he already had an inkling of the answer.

"The folk staying in the inner bailey come down, and pay me a half penny each for a half hour with one of the girls."

"What's Tad's role in this?"

"He fetches the pallets. That floor's hard and cold."

"Not to mention stony," Stephen murmured.

"And that, too. You've been in there?"

Stephen had in fact been in the tunnel as a boy. The tunnel led to a shaft that rose to the northwest tower's ground floor, which was used as a storeroom, dank, musty, and filled with barrels and sacks. It had always been a good hiding place for squires looking to shirk their duties. The hatch sealing the shaft was locked, but those who knew someone could get the key. This had been at least fifteen years ago, but he doubted anything had changed. He asked, "So you were there Thursday night?" That was the night Ormyn disappeared.

Thumper nodded.

"The whole night?"

"Most of it."

"And when you left, you found Ormyn's body?"

"Not exactly."

"Please don't keep me guessing. It is very tedious."

"We were doing our business when about midnight some rough sorts came to the grate. Some lads from the army, I think. Scared the hell out of me, I'll tell you."

"Will, I'm surprised you're scared of anything."

"Well, they had swords and axes." Thumper squinted as he sought his memory. "And, strange, one of them had a shovel. Banged it on the grille. I've no idea why anyone would bother with a shovel that time of night. But I don't like to argue with such folk. And the grate was unlocked, you see. They could have come right in. But they stayed outside. Just told us to stay put and say nothing to anyone. Otherwise, there'd be hell to pay. They knew who we were and what we were up to. I don't know how they knew, but they did. Said they'd find us and cut our throats."

"How many of these rough folk were there?"

"Seemed like a dozen, at least. But it was dark and hard to tell."

"What happened after they came to the grate?"

"Like I said, one remained there, keeping an eye on us. The rest went round the corner. I heard them talking now and then, low like, so I couldn't make out what they were saying. Then there was a crash and a thump. A little bit later, they all went away."

"Which way?"

"They went downhill, toward the path to Dinham Bridge."

"A crash and a thump, you said."

"It was that fellow Ormyn."

"A good guess on your part, I suppose. Then what did you do?"

"They said to stay a full hour. But we left right away."

"But not before going to see what made the crash and thump."

"Well, no."

"No?"

"I'm a prudent man. I take no notice of thumps in the night that don't concern me. We were making our way along when we heard a groan. Tad went up to see what it was. He's like a dog, sometimes that boy, always poking about in things he ought to leave alone. He found that fellow lying there in the bushes. Now I wish he hadn't."

"Ormyn wasn't dead?"

"Not right then. But he died soon after."

"Did he say anything about what happened?"

"No, he wasn't conscious, and hardly breathing, in fact, by the time we got to him, just doing those little hiccup-like things that people make when they're dying. I had my finger under his nose to make sure when he stopped."

"What happened to his purse and clothes?"

Thumper shuffled his feet, not eager to address this question. But at last he said with a sigh, "We got 'em."

"You stripped a dead man who wasn't even cold."

"I didn't. I had the girls do it."

"You have no shame."

"People do say that about me. I take pride in it."

"Do you still have his things?"

"Oh, yeah. Haven't tried to sell any of it yet."

"Waiting for the controversy to die down?"

"Something like that."

"Well, don't."

"Don't what?"

"Sell them. I'll be back for them. They belong to the widow now. And Ormyn's sword — do you have that as well?"

"We didn't find no sword. Funny thing, now that you remark upon it. He had a belt and scabbard on him, but the scabbard was empty."

Chapter 8

The girl Cicely's house lay a quarter mile down the Galdeford Road from Thumpers', a small hut surrounded by budding oak and elm. A man and boy were sawing boards from a log, the boy on top of the scaffold and the man in the pit beneath. A pile of logs and fresh boards lay beside the pit, indicating that the profession of the householder was a sawyer.

The boy called "Dad! Visitor!" alerting the man in the pit as Stephen pushed through the gate in the wicker fence about the yard, and the man climbed out of the pit. Rather than looking abashed, they looked angry at having been discovered to be working on a Sunday.

"What can I do for your?" the man asked, adding a "sir" at the end after a long pause. "You don't look like anyone from the parish. You in the market for some timber?"

"I'm looking for a girl. Name of Cicely."

The sawyer sucked on his front teeth. "What makes you think we've a girl by that name here?"

"Will Thumper said she lived here."

"Thumper?" The sawyer frowned. "That son-of-a-bitch big mouth. He told you where to find her?"

"Yes."

"Anything for a fucking penny. What do you want with her? She's done with that business."

"I just want to ask her a few questions."

"Questions?" This proposal seemed to dumbfound the sawyer. "What about?"

"The dead man."

"What dead man?"

"The one found yesterday outside the castle."

"What makes you think my girl knows anything about that?"

"Because she was there, with Thumper, when they found him."

"I thought it was a bunch of boys who found him."

"I've already been to Thumper's. He told me all about it."

"Then what do you need my girl for?"

"Do you believe everything you hear from Thumper?"

"No."

"Neither do I."

"Are you that coroner fellow? Attebrook?"

"That's me."

"Heard of you. Just a moment." The sawyer retreated round back of the hut.

He returned a bit later with a young girl. Stephen was shocked to see that she had to be no more than twelve or thirteen.

"She'll talk to you," the sawyer said, "but only on condition that her name don't come up in connection with this."

"Fair enough. I've no interest in what business you two engage in after dark."

The sawyer prodded Cicely forward. "Have your way, then."

If Stephen expected a saucy girl, he was disappointed. This was a little mouse, with wiry brown hair showing from beneath her cap, gentle eyes, and receding chin. She kept her eyes on the ground, hands folded upon her stomach, the fingers tangled together. She looked embarrassed to be here, her father embarrassed as well, which he tried to cover up with an air of belligerence.

Stephen was uncertain how to start. He felt as though some delicacy was required, since whoring out your daughter had to be a touchy subject for most people. But he lacked subtlety, an aspect of character than had frustrated his former master, the crown justice Ademar de Valence. ("You're too much of a lout even to make a living collecting shit in a wagon!" de Valence had once shouted at him after some now forgotten mistake.) His normal approach was a brash lunge forward, heedless of fine distinctions or people's feelings. And as he struggled for a way to begin, his mouth took things in hand for itself: "Will Thumper said you're one of the girls he takes up to the castle."

Cicely nodded, eyes on the ground. A blush had begun to creep up her neck.

"You were there when Tad found the dead man."

Cicely shook her head.

"I know you were."

After a false start, Cicely said in a whisper, "I wasn't there. I came along after."

"Right. You were in the tunnel."

Cicely nodded.

"But you saw him."

Cicely nodded.

"Was the man still alive?"

Cicely nodded.

"Did Thumper do anything to hasten the fellow's death?"

Cicely coughed. "No. He died right after I got there. Just gave up the ghost. You're not thinking we had anything to do with it?"

"Just being sure. And then you stripped him."

"Will made us do it. I didn't want to." Cicely shuddered and wiped her hands on her skirts.

"There were some men who came to the grille of the tunnel, did you see them?"

Cicely nodded.

"About what time?"

"Middle of the night sometime, I don't know."

"What did they look like?"

"I don't know. It was dark."

"You had a candle."

"The candle was by the ladder, with Will."

"The ladder . . . ah, you mean the ladder leading up from the tunnel to the cellar of the tower."

"Right," Cicely said. "It was dark outside. I just heard them moving around and talking. Gave me a bit of a fright. I thought they'd try to get in. The grille's not locked back up till we leave."

"How many?"

"I don't know. Two, three maybe."

"Besides the men at the grill," Stephen said, "did anything else unusual happen that night?"

"There was the dead man. But that was in the wee hours, really."

"Besides that, anything else that seemed unusual?"

"Well, there was the man who went out."

"A man went out? When?"

"I don't know. Sometime after those fellows made a racket at the grille. I can't remember." She added, "What was really unusual about it is that he paid Will at the ladder, then just slipped out without taking part, you know, in any of us girls."

"Did you get a look at him?"

"At who?"

"The man who went out."

"No. I had a customer on me then. I heard him talking to Will, and then he walked by, tripped on me leg, he did. I keep my eyes closed usually, you know, when I'm engaged. It's easier that way. It don't do much for the smell, though."

"So you heard him?"

"Clear as a bell, even over all the grunting that was going on. That's one rusty grate."

Ludlow Castle had two chapels, the round one in the inner bailey which was dedicated to Saint Mary Magdelene for the elite and a small timber one that looked like a hut more than a place of worship in the outer bailey for the servants. This little timber chapel stood against the north wall, its neighbors a barn, a pig-sty, a vegetable garden, and for the moment a vast tent covering piles of hay for the horses of the army's knights and mounted sergeants in the temporary paddock nearby. This did not leave much space for the crowd which had come to pay its respects to Ormyn Yarker and his family. The crowd was so large and so densely packed that several mourners were propelled through the fence defending the vegetable garden, but fortunately, the wives who tended the garden had anticipated this sort of trespass, and they were on watch, encouraging those clumsy folk to retreat with the help of staves and firm warnings.

As a consequence, it took Stephen more than half an hour to find Gilbert in order to share what little he had learned in Lower Galdeford, and he only happened to make the connection on his second circuit by the barrels of ale set up by the chapel's door when he spotted Gilbert's head above the crowd: he was standing on a box which teetered so that he seemed likely to fall into the pigs' run. All it would have taken was a slight nudge and over he would go. A pair of boys were eyeing Gilbert for just such a pitching when Stephen arrived at his side and sent the boys away with a glare.

"Ah, there you are!" Gilbert said, although with the noise of a thousand conversations at once, Stephen could only guess that's what he said from the movement of Gilbert's lips.

"What?" Stephen said as he grasped Gilbert by the sleeve to save him from falling among the pigs, which were lined up by the fence because people in the crowd threw them morsels of food. They enjoyed seeing the pigs scramble for the morsels. Pigs are not stupid, and they put on quite a show, which encouraged the throwing of yet more morsels.

"I said, there you are!" Gilbert said after he had hopped down.

"What?"

Gilbert pulled Stephen's head close to his so he could shout in Stephen's ear. "I said, where have you been?"

"I've been to see Will Thumper!" Stephen rubbed his ear and shouted back.

"What for, in God's name?"

"What?"

And so the conversation went, Stephen sharing what little he had found out and Gilbert asking clarifying questions. Stephen was glad for them although they often challenged his own views, but he was mindful of his impulse to leap to conclusions; "Evidence is hard!" his old master Ademar de Valence used to say. "Speculation is easy!"; advice he had not heeded until he had come under Gilbert's wing. The whole was punctuated by a lot of "what's?" — not a satisfactory way to make a report on an important subject, even if there wasn't much to it to begin with.

During the course of this discussion, they worked their way to the edge of the crowd, where the noise wasn't quite so bad.

Gilbert put fingers in both ears and rubbed vigorously. "I didn't even know there was a tunnel."

"I think it's been there since the castle was built, a secret way out, I suppose. I can't see it being much use as a sally port."

"I should like to see it some time."

"Few are allowed in."

"Yet you managed, apparently."

"When I was a squire here, we stole the key. There isn't much to see. A shaft so narrow the likes of you would probably get stuck in it descends from the cellar of the tower to the tunnel, which runs about thirty yards or so before it emerges on the hillside."

"And Thumper's been using it as a trysting place, to whore out the village girls?"

"Seems so."

"You can't imaging he's doing this without Turling's approval!"

"I reckon Turling gets a piece of it. I would if I were him."

"Which means there was probably quite a bit of coming and going to the north tower throughout the night. Yet no one saw anything untoward at the chapel. Nor even told us about it!"

"Yes," said Stephen, who had not thought of this, as his mind had been more on the problem of Ormyn's death than on the disappearance of the relic; although he acted as if he the thing had already occurred to him. "But all that coming and going could have concealed the movement of the thief. People might have thought that he was just another reveler."

"That is a possibility. All this is not helpful."

"No, it isn't."

"Well, come on," Gilbert said, taking Stephen's arm. "You should pay your respects to the family before you are trampled to death. They are just over there."

Just over there meant a mere forty or fifty yards, but it was a space packed with mourners who were reluctant to give way, so that another quarter hour elapsed before Stephen finally came face to face with the bereaved. Confronting the survivors was never a duty he relished, and he had done a lot of that lately. He would have avoided this if he could, but Gilbert had left him no option.

Ormyn's widow should have been by the cart carrying the coffin. But she was not in evidence. Only Ormyn's children were where they should be, a boy of twelve who was apprenticed to a weaver in town, and two girls, one eight and the other six. They stood by the cart, their faces sad, tear tracks on their cheeks. Stephen did the best he could, which amounted to "Sorry for your loss" and "He was a good man" and then bursting out of its own accord the cringe-worthy "Hope you're doing all right," which elicited brief smiles and nods. It was an awkward moment, but soon over.

That task behind him, Stephen breathed a little easier. He acquired a cup of ale, and had a deep drink to calm his mind, which took more time than he liked after his words with the children.

Gilbert wanted to lead Stephen in search of the widow, but he had had enough of comforting the bereaved for one day, and he begged off with "I've had enough. I'm going."

"What?" Gilbert shouted back.

When Stephen did not repeat himself, Gilbert followed along, although leaving the wake meant sacrificing free food and drink.

Stephen's luck, however, brought him to a goose pen at the edge of the crowd, where he was startled to find Bridget

Yarker. She was with a group of girls as young as herself, most of them unmarried. They were amusing themselves by throwing tidbits of bread to geese in the pen. Perhaps this was a more genteel thing for girls to do than amuse the pigs. There were a few lads with the girls, and one older man, Simon Jameson, another member of the castle guard. Bridget cast a crust into the pen. She turned to laugh with the others at the resulting scramble. Simon grasped her arm in a possessive way. Bridget disengaged herself and her lips moved so that Stephen made out, "Not here, not now." Simon looked put out. But Bridget brought him out of his pout by saying something in his ear. They smiled at some secret, their heads together for a moment before they drew back.

"Something is not right about that," Gilbert said to Stephen. "Did you see it?"

"I saw something, I'm not sure what," Stephen said, relieved that Gilbert was so distracted by this perception that he did not insist that Stephen console the widow as well. It would have been a shame to interrupt her fun with trite mutterings about loss and such.

"Most new widows of my acquaintance are not so happy. It is usually a disaster to lose a husband, but she seems rather relieved."

Stephen reflected that Gilbert was right about this. He had met quite a few newly minted widows in his time, and he could not recall one who had been so unconcerned by a husband's death, even when the marriage had not been a success. "Some cuckolding going on before poor Ormyn's fall, perhaps?"

"I wouldn't be surprised. I wonder what Simon Jameson was up to Thursday night."

"Hmmm, it wouldn't be the first time a jealous lover disposed of a rival. At the behest of the wife, perhaps?"

"I shall be disappointed if that is true," Gilbert sighed. "She is such a pretty thing, so young, so fresh. I hate to think she's capable of murder. But we must keep in mind the example of Margaret de Thottenham to remind us. A pretty package can just as easily conceal a hard heart as an ugly one."

"Let's leave Margaret out of this."

"You must admit that the sight of you leaping through a window when she tried to have you killed was very funny."

"That was just a spat. We've patched up our differences, or don't you remember?"

"I wouldn't put it past her to do something like that again, if the need arose."

The best way to find out what Jameson was doing Thursday night was to ask the man. But that would require prying him loose from Bridget, since if they were in fact in league over Ormyn's death, it was best to question them apart from each other. Now did not seem to be the time, but then another way occurred to Stephen. He spotted another man from the garrison, and asked, "Have you seen Turling?"

The soldier snorted. "You can't be serious, sir. He'd not come out for this. He don't give a damn what happens to us. When his service is up, he'll be gone without a look backward." Turling was one of the lesser gentry, whose family was only a rung or two above Stephen's. He was not the permanent guard commander, instead fulfilling his knight service, whereas the guards themselves were hired soldiers whose complement did not change.

"He'd be in the inner bailey, then," Stephen said.

"I expect so, hanging around his betters and hoping to be noticed." As Stephen turned away, the soldier added, "We're glad you came, sir. It means a lot, it does."

Gilbert pulled up short when Stephen veered toward the round chapel of Saint Mary Magdelene within the inner bailey rather than taking the stairs in the gate tower to the guard commander's quarters. "Why are we going there? I thought we were after Turling."

"I've just thought of a few more questions for our monks. I want to ask them before I forget."

"You won't mind if I find something else to do?"

"You don't fancy another confrontation with Brother Adolphus?"

"He never was my favorite person, no."

"All right, then. Why don't you hunt down Turling and ask him if Jameson was on duty Thursday night."

"I'd think you're better fitted for that. You know the man and can speak to him on the same level, more or less. But I, a lowly clerk and a merchant besides? You recall his attitude."

"Well, if you have no appetite for Turling, you could just linger by the door, where you might be seen by your former friends."

"There is that. Very well, if Turling's my alternative."

"You are such a good fellow," Stephen said in an overly hearty way. "With you on the case, we shall find the answer to Ormyn's death in short order. I should like that load off my mind. The other is heavy enough."

"Good fellow! You say good fellow to me? You are becoming decidedly cheeky. It shows that you're spending far too much time under Harry's influence."

Stephen pointed to the gate tower, which they had just passed through. "I'd start there. The boys should have some idea where he is if his wife doesn't."

"I shall inquire. I am very good at inquiring, as you know." Gilbert swung around and made for the tower, glad to get away from the chapel.

"As I know," Stephen murmured to Gilbert's back.

Stephen entered the chapel. There was no one inside, so he crossed through the chancel to the temporary dormitory in the scriptorum. He supposed he should knock, but he didn't. Some of the monks were packing their few belongings into satchels. This seemed an odd thing. Few travelers set out for anywhere this late in the day, much less go anywhere on a Sunday.

"May I help you, sir?" the closest monk asked.

"I'd like to see the prior."

"He's not feeling well. I'll fetch Brother Adolphus."

Brother Adolphus was visible at the rear of the dormitory sitting on his cot, reading a small book. He looked annoyed when the monk reached him and gestured at Stephen. Brother Adolphus marked his place with a blue ribbon and put down the book. He crossed the dormitory in no hurry to see what Stephen wanted.

"You have good news for us?" Brother Adolphus asked. "No, I suppose not. That would be asking too much."

"No, I have only a question or two."

"If you must."

"I understand the earl intended to give the relic to the Prince."

"That was his intention."

"And that it was the earl who had the emeralds affixed to it."

Brother Adolphus' mouth turned down. "He did that."

"And I suspect this gift was a secret. No one knew of it. But you, of course."

"The earl instructed us not speak of it."

"So it would be a surprise."

"Yes. A surprise."

"Did anyone other than you and your brethren — and the men at Wattepas' establishment — know about this plan?"

Adolphus shook his head. "Not that I know of."

"Are you sure there's no way anyone else could know that the relic had been . . . enhanced?"

"You mean desecrated? I cannot think of anyone."

"Did anyone else come in the shop while you were there?"

"I cannot remember. There might have been. Is this important?"

"I don't know. I say, are you leaving?"

"At first light tomorrow. I trust you'll send word if you find our missing relic." Brother Adolphus did not wait for a reply. He turned away and glided back to his cot.

Gilbert was by the gate when Stephen emerged from the chapel. "That was quick," Stephen said.

"He wasn't in. He's gone bowling, his wife said. Goes every Sunday. She said he seems to like his bowls more than Mass."

"A sore point between them?"

"Apparently. Did my old friends tell you what you wanted to know?"

"Brother Adolphus was not helpful." Stephen recounted their conversation.

"He said there might have been," Gilbert mused when Stephen was done. "That means there probably was. Wattepas is a busy man. People are in and out of his shop all the time." Gilbert drummed his fingers on the handrail of the drawbridge. "As it is Sunday, we shall find him at bowls as well and kill two birds with one stone. It is a bit of a walk. Are you up to it?"

"Are you insinuating something?" Stephen asked as they stepped off the drawbridge and headed toward the main gate.

"Not at all. Try to keep up with me. That's all I ask," Gilbert said.

"I shall do my best."

The land within the town walls was not flat enough for bowls, except perhaps for High Street or the castle bailey. But the bailey was impossible, of course, and High Street too rutted and full of pot holes. The stones would have flown off at all angles in the street, to the hazard of the buildings, not to mention pedestrians who got in the way. There was the graveyard at Saint Laurence's church as well, but the priests did not approve of gambling because of the wreckage it brought to so many lives, and there was a lot of that wherever there was bowls.

Yet all was not lost to the bowls enthusiasts, for an enterprising inn owner a few hundred yards north of Corve Gate had sufficient level ground for the game which had originally been dedicated to archery butts. A few of the butts remained, but bowls had taken over the rest of the yard. It was a popular spot where there was plenty of wine and ale (at much higher prices than elsewhere) and the soothing view of the River Corve close at hand, where there were tables under the trees, and one could sit in the shade, sip wine, and criticize the play. The riffraff made do with the field north of Linney Gate, where they competed for space with the wrestlers, the archers, laundry that some housewife had neglected to bring in, and the sundry horse out to graze.

It was almost warm enough now that one could do without a coat, unusual for March, and Stephen was actually sweating as they descended the road to the Pigeon Inn. He paused at Saint Leonard's chapel, which occupied the southern corner where Linney Street came in from the west, to wait for Gilbert to catch up. He was glad for a the rest, since his bad foot had begun to pang from all the walking. The inn lay opposite Linney Street from the chapel, and its front yard was filled with people enjoying the unexpectedly warm weather and the sun, which they hardly ever got to see. Although these were mainly soldiers who were encamped in the castle meadow and people who lived outside the town, and thus not the Broken Shield's natural prey, Gilbert regarded the crowd with envy, which broke into positive gloom at the sight of the large number of bowlers in the inn's back garden. There were six games going on at once and the tables along the river were filled.

"Do you think Edith would allow you to turn the Shield's back garden into a bowling alley?" Stephen asked.

"I wouldn't mind a bowling alley, but where would we put the woodpile and the privy? Besides, the yard's not flat enough. We'd have stones flying down to the river. Imagine the mess and confusion. Ah! There he is!" Gilbert pointed to a tall figure across the pitches just rising from a table. Leofwine Wattepas wiped his hands on a towel and strode toward one of the alleys. "We must hurry if we are to catch him."

Gilbert pushed through the gate and rushed toward Wattepas.

Wattepas had already taken up a black oval bowling stone and was eyeing his first cast at the wooden cone that was the target many yards away when Stephen caught up with Gilbert. Wattepas was taller even than Stephen, who towered over most men. He had massive shoulders and muscular arms that would have done a mason's apprentice proud, and large hands with thick fingers, not the sort you'd think suitable for a goldsmith whose work was often delicate and fine. He was in his middle forties, and already fully gray-headed with a thick mane that hung to his shoulders and a neatly trimmed gray beard that gave him a distinguished look. For a man whose wife was as sour as Lucy Wattepas, he was unexpectedly genial, with a smile that often lingered on his lips and sparkled his blue eyes.

"Well, Sir Stephen, Master Wistwode," Wattepas said, "ordinarily I'd say this was a pleasure, but you are clearly up to something, and that means hurt and despair are not far off. What can I do for you?"

"Sorry to interrupt your game, Master Wattepas," Stephen said. "I only have a few questions."

"It can't be about that unfortunate castle guard, can it? Or has someone else died since I left the house this morning? My wife hasn't murdered one of the servants, has she?"

"It's nothing like that. It has to do with your business with the monks of Greater Wenlock."

"Ah, that. I'm not at liberty to speak of it. Sworn to secrecy and all that. Could have my tongue ripped out, you know. The earl is a formidable enemy when crossed, although I think you already know that from your dealings with him."

"I'm afraid that you'll have to speak of it to us. We're charged with recovering the missing relic."

"I see. Probably not a task you relish, eh? Well, there's not much I can tell you. If you've spoke to the monks, you'll already know of my part in it."

"There are some things they do not remember."

Wattepas sighed. "I see there is no way I'll escape interrogation. Perhaps we could go somewhere no one can overhear."

He handed the stone to another player, and led Stephen and Gilbert to the banks of the river, but not before snaring a cup from a table.

"Mind holding this?" Wattepas asked Gilbert. He held out the cup to Gilbert. Then he unlimbered himself and began to urinate in the river.

"I say, Master Wattepas!" Gilbert exclaimed. "Not in the river. People drink that water."

"Oh, yes, well, some do, don't they," Wattepas said, not sounding much concerned but adjusting his aim to the base of a willow. He rearranged his clothes and recovered his cup. He upended the cup. "That's better. So, Sir Stephen, what is it you want to know?"

"You say neither you nor any of your boys spoke to anyone about the work done for Earl Percival."

"I didn't exactly say that, but no. No one spoke of it."

"You're sure."

"I certainly didn't, and I'd have the hide off any of my boys if they did."

"But you cannot be sure."

"I trust them. If I tell them to keep quiet about something, they damned well better keep quiet."

"Is there any possibility that someone else might have found out?"

"I don't see how." Wattepas stroked his chin. "Well, wait. A fellow came in the shop while the monks were there, now that I think about it. Monks in a goldsmith's shop are a novelty, as you can imagine, so he gave them the eye. But I don't recall that they said anything to him that gave the game away. They're a silent lot. Not much given to idle speech."

"Do you recall who that person was?"

"Never seen the fellow before. He was one of the lords who came at the summons. A lesser one, if his clothes were any indication." Wattepas' eyes wandered over Stephen from feet to the top of his head. "Better off than you are, though."

"Most people are better off than me."

"A pity. Such a well turned out fellow you are, too, sir. But I am aware of your . . . problem. So unfortunate."

"Does everybody in town know?"

"I'm afraid so. Hard to keep secrets in Ludlow, you know. Small town. Everybody knows everybody else's business. Fart green cheese and everyone will know about it by the end of the day."

"Except this."

"This? Oh, right. The bones. Strange they'd just disappear like that."

"Earl Percival is most distressed," Gilbert said.

"He must be, if he's engaged Sir Stephen to find them, after their unpleasantness last winter."

"It wasn't his idea," Stephen said.

"Randall put you up to it?" Wattepas asked.

"After Prince Edward assigned him the commission."

"Randall always likes to have someone else do his dirty work."

"I wouldn't say that," Stephen said.

"Of course, you wouldn't. A man can't speak ill of his lord, can he?"

"Not in public, although he's not my lord."

"Ah, yes, he's your employer. A different kettle of fish, but not that different, eh?"

"You haven't any idea of this fellow's name, do you?"

"No. I never spoke to the man."

"Did anyone?"

"One of my boys. I was too busy. Couldn't trust anyone else to fix those stones to the bones, you know. Delicate business."

"I'm sure it must have been."

"It required us to drill holes through them. For the pins, you see. You can't just paste that stuff on and expect it to stay for any length of time. You'd have thought I was drilling holes through the monks themselves, from the look of them."

"I understand they were distressed."

"I'll say they were. They wouldn't let me touch the bones with my bare fingers, did you now that? Had to wear gloves the whole time. You've no idea how that interferes with your ability to do close work."

"I can imagine."

"It must have been a tiny drill," Gilbert said.

"Of course it was a tiny drill!" Wattepas said. "I'm the only man within a hundred miles capable of such work! That's why Earl Percival came to me in the first place."

"I'm aware of your reputation," Stephen said.

"The things were a masterpiece when I was done," Wattepas said, "the settings, the stones, everything. Work that should live through the ages! Gone now!" He wagged a finger in Stephen's face. "You better find them, sir!"

"I'm trying. Which of your boys dealt with this person?"

"Wace over there," Wattepas said, pointing to a short black-haired man about Stephen's age standing at the edge of one of the bowling alleys, stone bowl in hand, waiting for his chance to cast.

"I shall speak to him then," Stephen said, "and let you get back to your game."

Wace cast his stone as Stephen and Gilbert approached. The stone rolled upon the grass, reminding Stephen of a wagon wheel that had come loose and taken off on its own. The stone passed the wooden cone, collided with another stone lying close by, wobbled, then fell on its side. Wace clapped a hand to his head and groaned.

"That's it, then," one of Wace's companions said. "You owe me tuppence."

Wace stalked by Stephen and Gilbert as if they weren't there and collapsed on a bench. He dug into his purse and tossed the coins at the companion. "I hope you choke on them."

"I'll be choking on wine!" the companion laughed as he pocketed the pennies.

"That's a lot to lose on a single bowl," Stephen said.

Wace regarded Stephen sourly. "It's not been my day."

"Can I buy you a drink?" Stephen asked.

Wace brightened at the offer. "I wouldn't mind that, sir."

"Gilbert," Stephen said, "please fetch this fellow a cup of wine, if you please?"

"Me?" Gilbert asked. "Why me?"

"You are my servant, after all."

"I am a clerk, not a servant."

"Well, you're carrying the money. Be a good fellow." The truth was, Randall had been slow with his wages again, and he had only a farthing left in his purse.

"It's easy to be generous with other people's money," Gilbert grumbled.

"I'll pay you back."

Gilbert made no move toward the inn, where the proprietor could be seen through the windows dispensing wine and ale in addition to his opinions about politics rather too loudly for his own good. Instead, Gilbert waved to draw the attention of one of the serving girls.

Stephen sat down beside Wace. He noticed Ralph Turling at the farthest bowling alley. Turling saw Stephen at the same time; he raised his cup and nodded. Stephen nodded in return. Turling returned to his conversation with a fellow bowler, who had a stack of coins on the bench beside them. Turling laughed and hefted his bowling stone.

"You're not here for the bowls or the drink," Wace said. "I saw you talking to Wattepas."

"No. This is the same old business, I'm afraid."

"I already told you I didn't work on them. That was the master. He didn't trust anyone else on a commission as delicate and important as that."

"So I gathered from him. I'm interested in a slightly different aspect of the matter. You attended a fellow who came in the shop while the monks were there."

"I did? I hardly remember."

"Think. It wasn't that long ago. Only last week."

"The days run together. We have so many people in the shop, especially now, with the army in town. It's hard to recall."

The fellow across the table who had won the bet with Wace must have overheard them. He said, "Come on, Wace. How could you forget that arrogant shit? It was that lord from the east."

"Was it, Oslar?" Wace asked. "I've quite forgotten." He accepted a cup from a serving girl who had come over. He downed the contents without pausing for breath. Movement upon Corve Street caught his eye, where a column of soldiers was trudging toward Corve Bridge. He looked alarmed and put down the cup. "Your honor, if you'll excuse me, I have some pressing business." He pushed through the gate and strode quickly toward Corve Street.

"You recall him?" Stephen asked Oslar, another journeyman, whom he remembered seeing in Wattepas' shop.

"He came in to sell some silver plate. Personal stuff. Even had a family crest on the bottom. Very eager to do it, too, by the bargain he accepted. We were able to get it for less than it's worth. Well made stuff, too. A pity to have to melt it down."

"He was there when the emeralds were affixed to the relic?"

"I'm certain of it. Wace here and I both waited upon the fellow."

"Did he show any particular interest in it?"

"No, I don't think so. Well, he did remark on how amazing the emeralds were. They were quite large, and enormously valuable. FitzAllen paid a small fortune for them."

"And you recall his name?" Stephen asked.

"Parfet was his name. Richard Parfet."

Chapter 9

"Can't this wait until later?" Ralph Turling asked.

"It can wait until you have made your cast," Stephen said.

Turling seemed to want to argue, but gave up the idea and nodded. He stepped to the pitch and cast his stone. It rolled toward the wooden cone, collided with it and fell on its side within inches of the target. Turling stepped back with a smile and said to his opponent, "See if you can do better than that!"

As the opponent stepped up to the line, Turling poured another cup of ale. "So, what do you want?"

"Can you tell me if Simon Jameson was on watch Thursday night?" Stephen asked.

There was an odd flicker of emotion in Turling's eyes: just there for a moment and then it was gone. Stephen wasn't even sure that he had seen it. Turling said, "Why do you want to know?"

"Humor me. It may be important, it may not."

"Of course, he was. He had the middle watch, same as Ormyn. Is there some connection?"

"I don't know yet. Perhaps. We shall see. Also, do you know a Richard Parfet?"

"I know of him. We've met a few times but have hardly spoken."

"Recently he sold much silver plate to Wattepas."

"Why is that a concern of yours?"

"I am curious as to why."

"I'd say it was none of your business."

"Still, would you have some idea?"

Turling shrugged. "He's in debt, why else? Everybody's in debt these days. It's damned hard to keep up appearances."

"Are his troubles more acute than ordinary?"

"I'd say that's probably the case if he's selling silver rather than pawning it."

Stephen rubbed his chin as he contemplated this. "But you have no first-hand knowledge of this?"

"Do you think Parfet pours out his troubles to me?" Turling asked. "Are you through? Can I return to my game?"

"Thank you, Sir Ralph. I appreciate your time."

In the armies of Stephen's acquaintance, the marshal and his deputies assigned the spaces for the tents in order to ensure adequate lanes and passages for traffic. But this army had come together haphazardly, and no such precautions had been taken, so the encampment in the outer bailey was a jumble. No one knew where anyone was, and it took more than an hour just to learn that Parfet had in fact been allowed to camp here rather than down below in the meadow.

"And were can I find him?" Stephen asked one of the deputy marshals, exasperated that what should have been a simple task was taking so long.

"Oh, he's gone."

"What do you mean, gone?"

"As in not here."

"But he was here this morning."

"So he was."

"But he is not now."

"That's what I said."

"Where did he go?" It was unbelievable that Parfet would have packed up and departed.

"He's been sent north. Left this morning."

"Where north?"

"Montgomery. You've heard of it, I assume," the deputy marshal said at Stephen's expression, which managed to convey incredulity and disappointment at the same time.

"Of course, I've heard of it."

"Are you finished? I have so much to do."

"I suppose this means we shall have to go to Montgomery, then," Gilbert said without enthusiasm. "Not a prospect I relish."

"Why would you think we need to go to Montgomery?"

"To question Parfet, of course."

"I was thinking of having him arrested and brought back here."

"Do you really think you could get the Prince to issue such an order?"

"He's eager for the return of the relic. Why not?"

"My boy, you've been caught up in enough intrigue already that you must have an inkling why not."

"I'm not sure I follow."

"Let me make it plain for you then. Parfet is a retainer of the Mortimers. If he is arrested and put to questioning, which will not be gentle, on the thin evidence we have, it runs the risk of offending Earl Roger Mortimer. Do you really suppose the Prince wants to take that chance, given the present political climate?"

"I was hoping not to have to make the journey as much as you."

Gilbert sighed. "No straight-thinking man would wish it. Montgomery is the veritable wilderness. Poking about there asking impertinent questions is a good way to get killed. If Parfet is our man, he'd just have to say we fell off horses, or the Welsh got us. Not a risk I would like to run."

"I would not want your death on my conscience. You can stay behind."

"And leave you to your own devices? Imagine the trouble that will ensue." Yet there was a note of relief in Gilbert's voice. "You'll have to be very careful."

"Perhaps there's a way to give myself some protection." He picked up the pace. Gilbert hurried after him.

"What, may I ask, is this plan?" Gilbert asked between gasps as they neared the gate to the inner bailey.

"And have you dash it with objections? You shall just have to wait and see."

"Oh, dear. This cannot be good."

With Prince Edward in residence at the castle, guards stood at the foot of the stairway leading to the door to the hall, admitting only those who had business with the magnates commanding the assembling army.

One guard conveyed Stephen's request to the occupants of the hall, while the other kept an eye on him and Gilbert. Presently, the guard returned and waved from the top of the stairs that the Prince had agreed to see him. Stephen climbed the stairs. Gilbert attempted to follow, but the guard above said, "Not you," and he settled back to wait some more.

A stone hearth, ten feet long by five wide, burned high in the center of the hall. The place was deserted except for a group of a dozen men seated about the table upon the platform to the right. Their voices echoed with talk about supplies and a shortage of wagons and horses to pull them, and a load of corn that had not come in from Birmingham as promised.

Stephen stopped at the edge of the platform and waited to be noticed. Finally Prince Edward motioned from him to approach. "Do you have anything to report?" Edward asked.

"I have a request, your grace," Stephen said.

"Oh," Edward said. The interest he had shown slipped behind a mask of politeness.

"I need a letter, your grace," Stephen said.

"A letter? What about?"

"A summons to Richard Parfet at Montgomery, commanding him to return to Ludlow."

Edward blinked. "Why do I need to summon Parfet? I need him where he is. The men in Montgomery threaten eastern Powys and preoccupy a large Welsh force which otherwise might be used to strengthen the array which I will face when I march. I cannot spare him."

"I need to question him. I cannot do it at Montgomery. He needs to be isolated from his friends. Otherwise, there is no hope of getting the truth from him."

"This is about the relic, is it not?"

"Yes, your grace."

"What's he got to do with it?"

"He may know something about what happened to it."

"I find that hard to believe. Why can't you just ride up there and ask him yourself? That's much easier than having him return."

"He can't because he is afraid," Percival FitzAllen said.

"Afraid of what?" Edward asked.

"Perhaps of being murdered."

"By Parfet? What nonsense!"

"It could prove dangerous for Attebrook to ride up there and ask questions that may be embarrassing," FitzAllen said. "If Parfet is our man." He smiled. "But then if Attebrook happens to die, that will give us our proof, won't it?"

Edward pursed his lips as he regarded FitzAllen, but did not speak immediately.

"At least give me the letter as a pretext," Stephen said, "so Parfet will know I come from you. That way he'll realize I'll be missed if I don't return."

Edward nodded. "All right, then. Just for him alone. He's to leave his men behind."

"Of course, sir."

"See my chancellor. He'll take care of you."

Chapter 10

Stephen did not expect to find a clerk handy since it was Sunday, but it turned out that the Prince was prone to dispatch letters at all times of the day and night. So at least one clerk had to be available to minister to his whims.

You would think that a simple letter like the one Stephen had in mind could be written quickly, but you'd be wrong. The clerk assigned to take down the letter either had wax clogging his ears or he was indifferent to Stephen's dictation, for it took three tries before the clerk had finished the letter to Stephen's satisfaction. Beyond the matter of phrasing, a sticking point was the clerk's insistence that the letter be in Latin rather than court French. "Proper letters are written in Latin," the clerk had said.

"I doubt Parfet reads Latin, or that there's anyone about him who does," Stephen said. "When the Prince writes to his commanders, doesn't he write in French?"

"I suppose he might. I don't know. I don't copy those letters. Wilfred over there, he takes care of those."

Stephen would have asked Wilfred's opinion, but he was asleep at his writing desk, which had been set up in what had been part of the guard room in the old hall of the gate tower. It seemed rude to wake him. Stephen stepped over to move an inkpot perilously close to the man's elbow. "Well, do this one in French, or I'll box your ears. I'm losing my patience."

The clerk was not impressed by the threat, but he composed the letter in French with only a misspelling and a grammatical error that had to be corrected, which meant copying the letter over again, since no mistakes could be allowed to mar a letter going out under the Prince's seal.

The Prince, of course, never saw the letter. The chancellor, sitting several places down from the Prince at the table in the hall, read it over and then applied the Prince's seal. "There you are," he said, handing over the letter.

"Many thanks, your honor," Stephen said.

"Don't thank me. Thank Prince Edward."

But Stephen did not have the opportunity. By the time he had his letter, supper had already begun in the hall, and he knew he would not be allowed to interrupt.

Stephen collected Gilbert at the far side of the drawbridge connecting the two baileys.

"Got your letter?" Gilbert asked. "Now we should find a notary and make out your will. You're going to need it."

"You have no faith in this plan?"

"Oh, yes, yes, plenty of faith. I am merely suggesting that you prepare for contingencies. Besides, once you are killed, a will should make disposal of your property less trouble. And you have your son to think of, after all. Consider what will become of him."

The mention of Stephen's son, Christopher, brought a pang of guilt. Last autumn, not expecting a war to break out between the English and the Welsh, Stephen had sent the boy, who was going on two now, to a distant cousin in Wales for what he had thought would be safe keeping. As a single man without prospects, he had no means of caring for a child himself. He had not seen the boy since then. "You are worse than Harry at making a person feel badly."

"Here, now, I am your conscience. Harry is merely a pest."

"A will." Stephen smiled slightly. "Now that you mention it, I should make provision for Harry. A few soap shavings should do the trick, don't you think?"

"I don't know why you would be compelled to do that, but Harry will like that, especially now that he has taken such a fancy to soap."

"Harry and soap. I'd never have thought to put the two words together until recently."

"Neither did I. You have created a monster, you know. God knows where it will lead."

Stephen had some idea already where it was leading. He wondered if Gilbert had seen the same things he had. He supposed not, otherwise he and Edith would put a stop to what was happening right under their noses.

They walked on in silence the rest of the way to the Broken Shield.

Supper had wrapped up, and a glance in the windows indicated that Edith, Jennie, and the servants were in a fury of cleaning, wiping tables, and sweeping floors. Gilbert ducked down so he could not be seen, but Stephen did not follow that example. Edith squinted at Stephen as he went on to the gate as if she suspected something was up. But she did not pause with her broom, and Gilbert made it safely to the yard without being called to some chore.

With supper over, there was no chance of getting anything to eat in the hall, so they repaired to the kitchen in the hope that there were leftovers, in this case white bean soup with a few carrots visible in the broth and smoked haddock.

"How I love smoked haddock," Gilbert sighed without conviction as they settled onto the bench outside the door to the stable alongside Harry, who was taking the sun.

"Haddock's better than cod," Stephen said, his mouth full of haddock. "Although it could use a little salt."

"It has too much salt!" Gilbert said, breaking his haddock in two and preparing to take a bite. "That's its problem! Enough to choke a horse!"

"That's unfair to the horse," Harry said. "Because it won't choke you. I love haddock, myself. Can't get enough of it."

"You shut up," Gilbert said, chewing glumly.

"What's got into him?" Harry asked.

"He's unhappy that I don't plan to put him in my will," Stephen said.

"What do you need a will for?" Harry asked.

"Because he's going off to die," Gilbert said, swallowing his wad of haddock.

"Why's that?"

Stephen explained what had happened during the morning and about the letter that lay on the bench beside him.

"Well," Harry said, lifting his cup, "here's to a swift and painless death, then. It's a good thing you've paid back the money you owed."

"Swift and painless deaths are always preferred," Stephen said, tucking into the bean soup.

"Yes, the other sort are such a bother," Harry said.

"What have you got there?" Stephen noticed what looked like his stirrup strap lying in Harry's lap. There was no sign of the stirrup iron. Instead, the strap seemed attached to a piece of leather.

"It's your stirrup, you idiot," Harry said. "What does it look like?"

"Not like any stirrup I've ever seen." Stephen picked up the strap.

"That's because it's been cunningly modified."

"Really?"

But the stirrup had indeed been changed. A shaped panel of leather had been attached with leather thongs across one side of the stirrup iron.

"I'd have used rivets, but I don't have any," Harry said. "I hope the ties hold."

"What's the point of the leather?" Gilbert asked, taking another bite of smoked haddock. "Keep off the rain?"

"That should be obvious, even to you. To keep his foot from sliding through the iron," Harry said.

"I shall have to try it out," Stephen said. He put the bowl to his mouth and drained the last of the soup.

He went into the stable and took down his saddle, which he draped on a sawhorse by the door. He attached the stirrup leather, and then climbed aboard the saddle from the right side as he usually did. Harry swung forward and guided his maimed foot into the stirrup.

"Hold on," Harry said. "It needs some adjustment. My, you have such big feet, even without your toes. I never noticed before. There, that should do it."

Stephen stood up in the stirrups. The iron on his left rested just before his heel, which is to say, about half way along what remained of the foot. This was too far back from where a stirrup iron should set. He felt the front of his boot pressing against the leather cap.

"Seems pretty secure," Stephen said, surprised at how good it felt, although he was not yet convinced it would do. "Thanks, Harry. What's this going to cost me?"

"Ah, yes, the price. I hadn't thought of that. I'll let you know after I've tallied my costs."

"Are you sure you have enough fingers?" Gilbert asked. "If you're forced to use your toes, you'll be in a pickle."

"I'll just borrow yours," Harry said.

"Gilbert!" they heard Edith call from one of the windows overlooking the yard. "Come here! You're needed!"

"Oh, dear," Gilbert said. "I've been found out. Coming, dear!"

"Nothing gets past Edith," Harry said as Gilbert retreated toward the inn. "She was just waiting for him to finish supper."

"I daresay, I have to agree with you for a change. Has she noticed what's happening between you and Jennie?"

"Nothing's happening between me and Jennie."

"Nothing? You're sure?" Stephen climbed off the saddle. "Well, let me know what this bauble cost you."

"You won't say anything about your suspicions?"

"They are, after all, only suspicions. It would not do to speak of them without proof. Unfair to the girl."

"Thanks, Steve."

"Don't mention it."

Chapter 11

Stephen had never been to Montgomery, and he had only a vague idea where it was: some thirty miles away to the northwest beyond Bishop's Castle. This made for a long day's ride, so he was up before dawn, dressed and packed, and in the stable saddling one of his mares. The commotion woke Harry, who clumped out of his stall, grumbling at being awakened, but who settled down when Jennie came out with a platter bearing their breakfast.

Jennie handed Harry several whole pennies, which he dropped in the begging cup hanging on a string around his neck. He in turn gave her something wrapped in a linen rag. She took pains to ensure that Stephen did not see what was concealed by the rag, muttering, "I hope you have a safe journey, sir," and with a glance at Harry fled back to the house. Harry watched her go with what Stephen thought might be wistfulness, but the expression vanished when Harry realized he was under observation.

Stephen settled on the bench beside Harry and ate leftover white bean soup, which was cold and thick as mud, but still surprisingly good for bean soup, while the mare and the stallion, which would serve as his pack horse, went at their oats. Horses did not like being put to work this early, but if they were well fed Stephen was less likely to get complaints from them.

They finished breakfast as the sky brightened. It was now just before sunrise and nearly time for the town gates to open.

"You know the way?" Harry asked, putting on the thick leather gloves that protected his hands.

"Well enough."

"They say that once you get past Ireland there's a great drop where the world ends."

"I'm not planning to go that far."

"You never know. Don't take any wrong turns or shortcuts."

"I'll be careful."

"Well, I'll be seeing you, then."

"Right," Stephen said.

Harry seemed about to say something further, but since the gates would open soon and he could not afford to miss the early traffic, he nodded and swung across the yard.

Stephen led the horses out of the stable.

He was just about to mount the mare when Gilbert and Edith emerged. Edith was carrying a small satchel. She held it out to Stephen. "To tide you over during the day," she said.

"Thank you, Edith," Stephen said. He put the satchel in his saddle bag.

Then he gathered the reins at the withers and put his left foot in the stirrup in preparation to mounting from the left rather than the right, as he had grown accustomed to doing. Gilbert's eyebrows rose at this and he seemed to hold his breath, as if expecting some disaster. But Stephen swung into the saddle, his foot safe and secure.

"I was anxious about that," Gilbert said.

"It seems to work well."

"I'm glad of that. You be careful."

"It's not going to be that bad. Don't worry."

"I hope so."

"There is something you can do while I'm away."

"What's that?"

"Look into the matter of Ormyn, if you will. Let's not let the trail get too cold. The army will be leaving in a few days, and our killer might go with it."

Gilbert glanced at Edith. "I shall ask around."

"Good. I shouldn't be more than a week."

Stephen turned the mare's head toward the gate to Bell Lane.

He rode up Broad Street with the stallion in tow, through the bull ring and toward Corve Gate, standing now and then while trotting just to get the feel of things. He would also have swung his sword about as well, but there were too many people watching for that.

Corve Gate was open by the time Stephen passed through it and headed down Corve Street toward the Bromfield Road. He felt content, despite his destination. It was always good to be on horseback going somewhere even if it might be into danger — especially if it might be into danger. He remembered the times he and his friend Rodrigo had ridden out on raids and occasionally to battle, and the laughter he and the others, who had been like brothers, had shared. All that was gone now, swept away by fire and sword. He wondered if he would ever experience such things again.

Corve Street curved gently right before its sharp bend in the distance where the road crossed the Corve, and as Stephen came round the bend he saw that a party of monks leading five donkeys occupied the road ahead. Stephen broke into a trot to catch up with them.

The monks of Greater Wenlock heard him coming and faces turned in his direction, then abruptly away. Stephen slowed up beside the lead donkey, which was being led by Brother Adolphus and ridden by the prior. Brother Anthony looked ill, his face ashen. He plucked at his habit and adjusted a string around his neck which was just visible beneath his collar, then pulled his hood over his head.

"Is the prior all right?" Stephen asked Adolphus.

"He's fine. Just a little under the weather this morning," Adolphus said, staring straight ahead.

"You're returning to Greater Wenlock?"

"That is our intent."

"But you're alone." Because of the unrest in the March and the frequent chance of robbery, most travelers chose to journey in parties of people heading in the same direction.

"We're anxious to be home."

"I could escort you," Stephen said. The route to Greater Wenlock was off his path to the northeast. He realized that the monks might not have been able to find anyone going in that direction.

"That won't be necessary. We've nothing of value. No one will bother us."

"You're sure?"

"Quite sure."

That seemed to exhaust Brother Adolphus' interest in conversation, and they marched on in silence.

As the road turned left to cross the wooden bridge over the Corve, Adolphus asked, "Where are you bound, by the way?" as if he was a bit startled that Stephen was still with them.

"Montgomery," Stephen said.

"What takes you there? The search for our relic?"

"Yes."

"An odd place to look for it."

"I go where the evidence leads."

"Hmm. Well, we shall pray you find it."

"Haven't you already done so?"

"Certainly. Of course we have. At every opportunity."

"I am glad of your prayers. I'm afraid that it might take a miracle."

"A miracle." Adolphus stared into the distance with a smile. "Yes. But Saint Milburga is quite capable of miracles when they are needed."

Two miles outside town, they arrived at the road to Stanton Lacy, which with the usual twists and turns of an English road ended up at Greater Wenlock. Without a word of good-bye or even good luck, the monks turned onto that lesser road and marched north toward the hills in the distance.

Stephen watched them go until they passed around the bend. He was alone. No one was upon either road or in the fields. If he was going to indulge himself, this might be the best place to do it. He tied the stallion to the branch of an apple tree growing by the road. He brought the mare to the center of the road and drew his sword.

He started with simple maneuvers, turning on the forehand and spinning on the haunches while remaining seated. He kept up these maneuvers, imagining he was surrounded by enemies who were trying to get behind him. Now and then he rose up in the stirrups and struck at these imaginary foes. Satisfied with this, he pushed the horse into a gallop up the road toward Greater Wenlock, standing as he raced onward, sword forward to pierce anyone who might get in his way. At the bend, he reined up and attacked a large silver birch growing by the roadside, cutting at the trunk but pulling the blows so they did not hit and damage his sword. He stopped after a short time so as not to tire the horse, for they had a long way to go.

He shortened the stirrup leathers by a couple of holes so that he would put more weight into the stirrups, keeping his bad foot more secure. It felt like old times, almost. He would never be completely whole, but for the first time since his wound, he did not feel so much a cripple.

Collecting the stallion, Stephen continued on to Bishop's Castle.

The road between Ludlow and Shrewsbury was wide and well-traveled, but the road to Bishop's Castle was little more than a cart track that wandered off to the west. Stephen recognized the turn because he had been down it before. It was the same turn he and Gilbert had made on their way to Clun during the winter. But Clun lay at the end of another turn-off about a quarter mile on, where the remains of a Roman road branched away, something to marvel at since it ran straight as a bow-shot, unlike the typical English road, which meandered like a drunken man on his way to the privy.

It was easy to get lost on such tracks. The land was sparsely settled here. There were no villages, nor even collections of hovels that might aspire to village status, just isolated houses on farmsteads here and there in the Welsh fashion. Occasionally, the track petered out to a footpath before resuming again, and there were frequent branchings which were the bane of any traveler on the lesser ways, since you could never tell which was the right fork. If you picked the wrong one, it would take you miles out of your way and add hours of toil to the journey.

The road climbed over hills and dipped into valleys, the way going higher and higher, woods pressing on either side, now and then opening to fields sometimes in wheat but often in grass and dotted with sheep, the herdsmen apparently heedless of the peril of the Welsh.

Stephen could have pushed the horses to make better time, since he was anxious to reach Montgomery, but he had not given any thought to the hills, which taxed the mare, and by the time the road dipped into the final valley and Stephen caught sight of Bishop's Castle in the distance, she was tired. Although he had a crick in his back and the usual sore bottom, he could have continued. But one had to be mindful of the horses and not abuse them. So even though it was midafternoon, he elected to spend the night. Twenty miles in a day would have to be good enough.

As a messenger of the Prince, he was entitled to a place at the castle, which saved on the expense of an inn and included supper and fodder for the horses.

In the morning when Stephen sought directions to Montgomery, one of the castle guards told him he had heard the night before while drinking in the town that a pair of Welsh drovers were returning there, wallowing in money, having sold a small herd of cattle to another man who planned to drive them to London. "There's not but one good road between here and there, though," the guard said, "so you can hardly miss it. But they'll be glad for the company. You might, too. They're a jolly pair. Never laughed so hard in my life."

Stephen was fortunate to catch the drovers at an inn off the market south of the castle before they set out, owing to the fact they slept late after the celebration of their success.

The pair proved to be a father and son who held land at Stanlawe, a village apparently not far from Montgomery, although the explanation was garbled by the fact that Stephen could only get Welsh out of the older man and the younger one was so hung over that he refused to speak in more than grunts. If they were glad for the company, they did not give any indication of it, nor of the good humor the guard had led Stephen to expect.

Since the drovers were on foot, it took more than three hours to reach Montgomery, where the lime-washed castle, brilliantly white in the spring sunlight, stood upon its high crag over the town.

Stephen learned from the castle gate ward that his quarry, Sir Richard Parfet, was not there. "Sir Richard was ordered to outpost duty," the ward said at Stephen's inquiry.

"Outpost duty? What does that mean?"

"He's gone to Old Montgomery."

"Old Montgomery? There's an Old Montgomery?"

"It's the old castle. Pretty much a ruin now, but it gives us a close watch on the ford of the Severn."

"How far off is it?" Stephen asked, hoping it would not mean he had a great distance to go. He was hungry and the time of day and the odors from the kitchen indicated that dinner was near.

"About a mile and a half. Take the left fork outside town. If you've a mind to, you can see it from the top of the west tower. It's the bump on the hill to the northwest."

"Watch for a bump on a hill."

"Something like that. Be sure not to miss it. If you keep going, you'll end up in Wales. You don't want that! The Welsh'll have your head off!"

"Thanks. As it's the only head I have, I'm anxious not to lose it."

Old Montgomery proved to be rather more than a bump on a hill when viewed close up, but it was falling into ruin, as the gate ward had warned. It was an old motte-and-bailey fortress of wood and earth that might have been grand once.

121

It had not one, but two encircling embankments topped by palisades. While perhaps this had meant strong defenses at one time, the outer walls were gray and rotten, showing gaps in places where the planks had fallen away and had not been replaced. Stephen noted these failings with a professional eye as he came around another ditched embankment to reach it. This neighboring enclosure had once contained a village, but there was nothing left of it but the remains of houses, some of which had been recently burned. The inner palisade of the fortress was in better shape, showing some sign of recent repair, yet even here the look of decay and neglect had not been dispelled. There were old posts jutting from the ground by the main gate which suggested towers had flanked either side, but the towers were gone now. Only a wall walk defended the gate from above.

The gate was closed, since it was only a little over a quarter mile from here to the Severn, which marked the border between Wales and England. So close, in fact, that it was easy to imagine mobs of screaming Welshmen rushing up the hill and catching people unaware, which perhaps they had done not too long ago, if the damage to the village was any indication.

A guard looked down at Stephen as he stopped at the gate. "What do you want?" the guard called down as he leaned on his spear, stroked his black moustache, and spat, the gob falling perilously close.

Stephen recognized the man as one of those outside the Spicers' wine shop, and he suspected he had been recognized in turn. He said, "A word with your commander, Sir Richard."

"What sort of word?"

Stephen was not used to being questioned so sharply by someone of a lower estate, and while he had lost just about everything, he still had some pride left. And a man having only pride to nourish him sometimes values it more than another man might. So he reacted more strongly than he might otherwise have done. "I carry a letter from Prince Edward for him, and if you don't open the gate right now, you disrespectful son-of-a-bitch, I'll climb up there and stuff it up your ass."

"He won't be able to read it then."

"It won't matter. I'll tell him what's in it."

"Dogface," the guard called back into the bailey, "get off that hay pile and open the gate. The boss has a visitor. Some toff who claims to be from the Prince."

There was a long pause, as if it took some effort for Dogface to rouse himself from that hay pile. Finally, the bar thudded and the gates opened, the iron hinges shrieking.

Dogface, another of the crew outside the wine shop, stood aside as Stephen rode into the bailey. There was no mistaking how he had got that name: although lean and hard, like any soldier, his jowls sagged beneath squinting eyes, giving him the appearance of an aging bulldog, except where most bulldogs had a mouthful of teeth, Dogface had only his upper canines, for someone had knocked out his upper and lower front teeth. Dogface looked Stephen over as he dismounted. "He doesn't look like a toff to me, Greg," Dogface said to the man on the wall walk. "Seems a bit . . . careworn."

"He talks like one," Greg said.

"You're a knight then?" Dogface asked Stephen.

"I am. Where's Sir Richard?"

"He's round the barn, yonder. By the chapel." Dogface gestured toward a small building that did not look very chapel-like, a corner of which was visible behind a square barn to the right. "It would be our chapel, sir," he added, "but we got no priest nor vicar. Godless bunch, we are." He winked and smiled, which did nothing to approve his appearance.

"See to my horses, if you please," Stephen said, handing Dogface the mare's reins and the stallion's halter rope.

Dogface had more sense than Greg to be disrespectful, especially since Stephen was in reach, armed, and armored, and had the look of a man who could do a lot of harm if he wanted to. It was easy to be insolent to strangers when you were eight feet above their heads; it was another thing when they stood right next to you with one hand on a sword pommel. But taking care of horses was beneath one even in Dogface's lowly state, and he shouted for a servant to come fetch the horses while Stephen marched around the barn.

Stephen heard women giggling as he reached the corner of the barn. He was taken a bit aback at this, since a frontier fortress was not a place where women were usually found, even among the servants. Stephen could think of only one good reason why they might be here, and his suspicions were confirmed as he came around the barn.

There were four of them, all young and all rather good-looking, and three of them, at least, still had their clothes fully on. One girl had her blouse open so that her breasts could take the sun and whatever attentions men hereabout might like to give them. She sat on the lap of a fellow with white blond hair who was gentry by the neat and combed state of his hair, his trimmed red beard, and the cut of his clothes. Two others sat on a log on either side of someone Stephen recognized; the name came to him as he stood there, Melmerby. The fourth girl was fumbling with a bowling stone, Parfet at her side. She paused from taking aim at the wooden cone which was the target of the game when Stephen came into view, and dropped the stone, just missing her feet. This brought a laugh from Melmerby and the blond man.

Parfet frowned at Stephen. He appeared peeved at the interruption. "Ah," he said. "I know you. You're Attebrook, from Ludlow, am I right? What are you doing here?"

Stephen advanced to Parfet, removing the letter from the waxed leather case that had protected it. "I was asked by Prince Edward to deliver this to you."

"So," Parfet said, "you are busy. A royal messenger, are you now?"

"I do what I am asked to do."

"Don't we all. Why on earth is the Prince writing to me?"

Stephen did not reply, other than to cross his arms and glance at the letter, which was now in Parfet's hands.

"What does he want?" the blond man asked as Parfet broke the seal and unfurled the letter.

"He wants me to return to Ludlow," Parfet said. "I'm to leave my men here and return straightaway."

"Just you?

"Yes, it seems he wants to question me about some stupid bones."

"I don't follow."

"A sack of some saint's bones went missing while we were there. It caused something of a stir."

The blond man waved a hand as if saint's bones were of no importance.

"What could the Prince possibly think I have to do with it?" Parfet asked Stephen.

Stephen shrugged.

Parfet tossed the letter back at Stephen. "Well, the Prince will just have to wait. I've more important things to do tomorrow than rush off about some silly old bones."

"What could be more important than a command from Prince Edward?"

"We're taking a ride in the country. You'll have to come along and find out, if you've the stomach for real soldiering."

Parfet's statement hung in the air. Real soldiering , he had said.

The prudent thing, given Stephen's suspicions, would be to insist that Parfet comply with the letter's command.

"Come on," Parfet said.

"What did you have in mind?" Stephen asked.

"The Welsh've burned several villages hereabout," Parfet said. "No doubt you've seen what they did to the few hovels remaining outside. I've a mind to pay them back and recover what they've taken. It's also a chance to make a little for ourselves."

"Besides," the blond man grinned, tweaking the whore's nipples, "it will be more fun than sitting on our asses around here. Not to mention profitable."

"You haven't spent much time sitting on your ass," the whore said.

"You hush," the blond man said. He pinched the girl again, and she squealed.

"It looks like you could use a bit of pillaging," Parfet said. "What do you say? One or two days, the Prince won't mind that."

"You mean a raid."

"He is a swift one," the blond man said.

"Let's be courteous, David," Parfet said. "Yes, a raid. You know, I was disappointed to be sent here, away from the army, but once I got here, David convinced me of the opportunities available at this post. We're both rather hard up for cash. Keeping up appearances is so difficult what with the prices of things the way they are today. But I don't need to tell you that."

"I am a bit hard up myself," Stephen murmured, as he digested the implications of this. Those emeralds were worth a castle or the rents from a town. If Parfet was so desperate for cash that he thought his best solution was to steal from the Welsh, then it was unlikely he had a hand in the theft of the relic. And if Parfet wasn't the quarry, who was? No one Stephen was likely to discover. If Stephen was unlikely to discover the thief, there was now only one course left to him if he wanted to avoid imprisonment, ruin, and possibly death at Percival FitzAllen's hands. Getting safely away required money he did not have. "They won't care if you do that? I thought you were supposed to watch the ford."

"We can watch the ford from the other side of the river just as well as we can from here."

"I suppose a couple of days won't matter."

"Excellent," Parfet said. "Say, how are you at bowls?"

Stephen was not any good at bowls, and by dinner time he was in debt not only to Parfet and the blond man, whose name was David Mably, but also to Melmerby, who was better at the game than any of them. Mably accepted his losses with reasonably good grace, even though Melmerby was Parfet's servant, a valet or chamberlain or something, as dinner was called and they abandoned the pitch.

For his part, however, Stephen was worried about his debt. "I haven't any money to speak of," he said.

"Don't worry," Parfet said, clapping him on the back. "We'll settle up after our adventure. Won't we, Melmerby?"

"Of course, sir," Melmerby said.

Chapter 12

Gilbert spent the better part of the day Stephen left trying not to think about what he had to do about Ormyn. It was not that he didn't want to solve the riddle of the castle ward's death. It was mainly that he had no more idea how to go about it than Stephen. He expected that inspiration would come in time, but by midmorning, when it became clear that inspiration was avoiding him, Gilbert forced himself to have thoughts about the problem. This did not help much. The only thing that came to mind was the canteen found at the foot of the wall. Stephen had done nothing about it. Perhaps, Gilbert decided, he should follow where it might lead. He was sure there was a connection. All this seemed like work. But there would be questions if Stephen got back, and Gilbert better have some answers, even if they were unsatisfactory.

So, he climbed the stairs to Stephen's room. It was four flights up, a garret at the rear of the house, and by the time he reached the top, he was gasping for breath. He had not made this climb for a long time. It was dark here, for no light penetrated the stairwell. He groped his way to the garret's door and pushed it open. With the shutters closed, it was hardly much lighter, until he crossed the room, stumbling on something on the floor, and threw them open.

It was normally used by the lowliest servants of the house. Narrow and small, with room for only a bed and a table beneath the window for a wash basin, the room overhead slanted so that a man Stephen's height had to stoop to avoid striking his head against the rafters except near one wall. Gilbert and Edith had given it to Stephen when he first arrived in the expectation that he would find it an insult and then go somewhere else; every room in the inn was precious and it was a waste to give it to Stephen even in payment of a debt to his brother. Yet Stephen had stayed without complaint. "I've slept in worse," was the only remark Stephen made about it. "At least it's got a roof. You could do something about that mattress, though." Gilbert was glad that Stephen had not left. He had got used to Stephen and Harry shouting to each other in the mornings before Harry left.

The object that had tripped Gilbert turned out to be the canteen. Why it should be lying in the middle of the floor was a mystery by itself, but he did not waste much energy seeking an answer to it. He retrieved the canteen and examined it more closely than he had before. He reflected again how expensive and rare an object it was: tin made and new, with hardly a scratch on it and no dents at all. Most canteens were leather. Gilbert turned it around in his hands. There was a maker's mark stamped on the bottom, the letters S and W intertwined, as there should be, for the thing was a work of art and the maker would have been proud of it and wanted people to know where it had come from. He had no idea who SW was. Nobody in Ludlow made such things.

Gilbert tucked the canteen under an arm. He was about to go when he noticed a folded piece of Italian paper on the bed. What need Stephen would have for paper, which was rare and expensive, was an even greater mystery than the canteen's position on the floor. Gilbert's hand hesitated over the paper. Could it be a letter to that beautiful but dangerous woman Margaret de Thottenham with whom Stephen was foolishly infatuated? If it was, Gilbert should leave it lie, but his curiosity triumphed, and he unfolded the paper. There was a crude drawing upon it that was unmistakably a sword hilt. The cross was curved toward the blade rather than straight, as in most swords of his acquaintance, and the pommel was tear-shaped rather than a round disk, the more common design, with grooves of some sort etched in it.

He put a finger to his lips as the significance of this drawing suggested itself. Stephen had said Ormyn's sword was distinctive. Here Stephen had tried to capture what it had looked like, undoubtedly to show to people. He had done the same with the likeness of Rosamond, the girl in the ice, so the same idea must have occurred to him now.

"Why did he not tell me about this?" Gilbert wondered, as he closed the door and went downstairs. The answer to that question was not pleasing: "Because he did not really intend me to make a serious inquiry after all. Well, I'll show him."

When Gilbert reached the meadow north of the castle where the bulk of the army had camped, his inquiry was frustrated by the fact men and women were rushing around packing things and loading carts. Nobody wanted to be bothered with him and it took several inquiries before anyone paid the slightest attention. Persistence at last forced a sergeant to turn from the urgent business of cart loading as Gilbert asked what was going on, and got the reply, "We're marching tomorrow. I'll bet you townies are glad of that."

"It will be more peaceful, that is certain," Gilbert replied. "I say, have you ever seen this before?"

The sergeant gazed at the canteen which Gilbert held out for his inspection. "No. You want to sell it?"

"Not at all. Someone lost it. I'm trying to find its owner."

"You are a Samaritan," the sergeant said, turning away to shout at a pair of soldiers manhandling a cask of arrows into a wagon which they had stacked in a way that did not satisfy the sergeant, although it was hard to tell what was the matter.

"Well, it is rather important that I find him," Gilbert said to the sergeant's back. "A matter of a man's unfortunate death, you know."

But the sergeant did not turn around, caring more for the loading of his wagons than someone's death. The reason for that became apparent when a knight strode up, glanced at the job the sergeant and his men were doing, and stopped. The knight's face got as red as his floppy hat. He threw the hat on the ground, and began shouting about the arrangement of the barrels, the gist of which was: "You've buried the wine casks, man! We'll not be able to get to them on the march!" This provoked the sergeant to sputter orders so fast that the words ran together so he could hardly be understood, as he spoke with a Devon accent, apart from the fact that most that came out were curses. The soldiers scrambled to comply with speed they had not exhibited until the appearance of the officer.

"I shall leave you to it, then," Gilbert murmured, turning away, but not without some admiration for the sergeant's performance.

He met no greater success elsewhere on the field. Many marveled at the canteen's workmanship and immediately recognized its value, but no one had seen its like before, or that of the sword on those times that Gilbert remembered to pull the picture from his pouch. By this time, people were settling down for dinner, the air choking with the smoke of cooking fires that accented the aroma of fresh bread and boiled beef, and he was reminded that he was far from his own dinner and unlikely to get back before the best stuff had been eaten. He had discovered this was a constant problem about investigations: they were tedious and dull, and he often missed his dinner. He might not enjoy the tedious and dull, but he was accustomed to them. However, missing dinner was not something he reconciled to easily.

Gilbert felt that he had exhausted the possibilities of the field and was heading back toward Linney Gate, imagining the delights of mutton stew, when he crossed paths with an ale-seller named Batson carrying a cask on his back as if it was a pack.

Batson had a collection of leather cups dangling from straps attached to the bottom of the cask, swinging about as he walked. The two of them halted as they came together amid the hubbub of the camp. For Gilbert, this hubbub had proven to be a source of dismay, but for an enterprising man like Batson, it was an opportunity. "Morning there, Gil," Batson said. "What brings you out here? Somebody die?" He cackled at his little joke.

Gilbert ignored the joke. He got the same from everyone. It was old and stale, and had not been funny the first time he'd heard it. "As a matter of fact, yes."

"Anybody I know?"

"That fellow at the castle — Ormyn."

"Oh, yes. The ward fellow, the one who jumped off the wall."

"Or was pushed. You knew him?"

"I knew who he was. Not that we were friends, or anything. Used to see him quite a bit down at the Pigeon, especially on Sundays when we made deliveries there. Care for a drink?"

Gilbert had not realized until this moment how much investigating made one thirsty. "Don't mind if I do." He eyed the dangling cups with some suspicion, however. No telling who had drunk out of them or when they had last been washed. He brought up the canteen, pulled out the stopper, and sniffed the contents. As he had suspected, the ale within the canteen had gone sour; ale never kept more than a few days. He poured it out, and handed the canteen to Batson. "Use this, if you don't mind."

"I'm not filling it up, mind you, unless you want to pay extra."

"A cup-worth's fine. Say, have you ever seen this canteen before?" Asking Batson was a long shot, but as Gilbert had decided to give up on the canteen, he might as well make it.

He was thus surprised when Batson answered, "Sure. I've seen it before."

"Where?"

Batson waved toward the east as he handed the now partly filled canteen back. "There, at the Pigeon."

"The Pigeon?" Gilbert had not expected this. "Not here, or the castle?"

"A fellow just leaving stopped me at the gate as I was making a delivery."

"What sort of fellow?"

"One of the soldiers. They'd just come in the day before. Not local folk."

Gilbert sipped from the canteen as he gathered his thoughts around this new and unexpected information. The ale was fresh and sweet. "This is good, Batson. Your wife is an artist. You don't happen to remember the fellow's name?"

"What fellow?"

"The owner of the canteen."

Batson snorted. "'Course not. I don't bother with people's names."

"Do you remember what he looked like?"

Batson's brow furrowed. "Can't say that I do. It's been a while."

"How much of a while?"

"Sunday before last, it had to be. I can hardly remember what my children look like. You can't expect me to remember some fellow I sold ale to out of this flock."

"I suppose not." Gilbert capped the canteen. "But you remember this."

"It's hard to forget a piece of work like that. How many people have a tin canteen?"

"Hardly anyone."

"And I remember that he had me fill it up. It holds a lot of ale. Hard to forget that, or the workmanship that went into that thing. T'is a thing of beauty."

"Thank you, Batson. You've been most helpful." Gilbert tried to sound grateful, but this news meant that he had lost any chance of fresh mutton stew.

"My pleasure," Batson said. "Oh, I remember something now about that fellow. I can't see his face but he had a great big moustache. Quite an impressive thing. You could hang laundry from it."

"You don't happen to remember the color?"

"Oh, sure. Black."

"Thank you, Batson. You've been a great help." Though at what was not clear, exactly.

They parted company then, Batson to continue business, and Gilbert to trudge toward Linney Lane, the prospect of more tedious inquiries stretching before him.

One would not expect the bowling field at the Pigeon Inn to be active in the middle of a weekday, but these were not ordinary times. There were half a dozen games going on when Gilbert pushed through the gate. While the Pigeon sought a higher class of customer than most bowling alleys, its owner was not the sort to turn anyone away with sufficient coin to pay the fee, but today the players all were gentry folk — officers of the army by the look of them, who had taken quarters at the inn in preference to sleeping in a tent, which they would have enough of soon now that Prince Edward had determined to march into Wales. Gilbert supposed the men were enjoying their last opportunity for leisure before the hardships of campaigning set in.

He went round to two of the groups, but despite the fact he asked in his most obsequious way, he was so sharply rebuffed each time that he hesitated to approach the third game. He was nerving himself up for another sharp rejection when one of the serving girls arrived at his elbow. "Drink for you, Master Gil?" the girl asked.

"No, Sally," Gilbert replied, swirling the canteen, which still held ale.

"Bring your own?" Sally asked, glancing at the canteen. "Better not let Herb see that. He'll have it out of your hands in a blink." She looked toward the house in case the owner, Herbert Jameson, was watching. "He don't like folk bringing their own."

"I can imagine why. Cuts into his profit."

"What are you here for? You didn't come for the drink or the bowls, that's clear."

"I'm looking into the matter of Ormyn's death."

"That ward at the castle? What a shame. He was a nice fellow."

"You knew him?"

"A bit. He used to come down, Sundays, and play. When he wasn't playing he'd cry on my shoulder."

"Something bothering him?"

"He had wife trouble — although I'd done more than enough to warn him about her. But he was an infatuated fool, like most men led about by his balls rather than his head."

"He was unhappy in his marriage, I take it?"

"Got that right, governor. See, Bridget's a demanding bitch. Everything's got to be her way, or there's a crisis, screaming and crying, sometimes rolling on the ground, mouth all frothy, or worse, the steady peck-peck-peck of her whining. Mind you, she pulled that a few times here on Herb, but he knew how to handle it. He just walked away and left her to talk to herself. But Ormyn, he was desperate that if he didn't please her, she'd leave him. And he couldn't stand that possibility. Yet no matter what he did, it was never enough. She was always picking at him about something."

"A marriage made in heaven." Gilbert sighed, thinking about how lucky he was. Edith was demanding too in her own way, but somehow they managed to get along without the dramatics.

"More like in hell. That was bad enough, but she's got a wandering eye."

"Oh, dear, you don't mean she —"

"I'm not sure whether she was just a horny lass. There are quite a few of those about, you know. Or whether she was looking for another situation. But at any rate, Ormyn suspected her. It drove him mad."

"You don't have any idea who her paramours might have been?"

"Only one. Simon Jameson. Turned out to be true, too. Bridget moved into Simon's house the day after the funeral. The idiot — he's been warned about her too, and it did no good."

"Good Lord, that is rude."

"Rude!" Sally slapped her thigh, laughing. "Got that right. She don't care about anyone's opinion except her own, I'll say that for her. Takes real stones to ignore community feeling."

"I had no idea, but then I have been rather busy investigating murders and the theft of valuable relics. Say, you haven't seen this before, have you?" Gilbert held up the canteen.

"Nah. You might go ask Herb about it, though, since he snatches them first thing as he sees them. If anybody brought it round, he'd know."

Herbert Jameson was in the kitchen disciplining a kitchen boy, who was cowering in a corner while Jameson beat him with a strap. Most of the blows landed on the boy's forearms, which protected his head. Jameson, a large and powerful man, was striking with such force that Gilbert almost intervened. Jameson glanced from Gilbert to the boy.

"Get back to work!" Jameson snapped.

As the boy scuttled to a large bucket filled with soapy water and pots, Jameson turned his attention to Gilbert. He wiped square hands on his apron, then fingered his square jaw as a question formed in his eyes. He was more than a head taller than Gilbert, with a square face to match his square hands, a broad nose, and a dome as bald as Gilbert's, although Jameson affected to comb part of his hair over the dome.

"Wistwode," Jameson said. "What brings you here? Spying on your competition?"

"Hardly. This is official business."

"What official business could bring you to my house?"

"The death of Ormyn Yarker ."

"What? I've got nothing to do with that."

"Nobody said you did. But you may have knowledge useful in finding his murderer."

"I find that hard to believe. Can we do this some other time? I'm rather busy."

"As am I. And no. We'll do it here and now."

Jameson looked as though he wanted to stomp away. But he stood still with some effort. "All right. Make it quick. I don't want you stealing any of my recipes."

Gilbert held out the canteen. "Can you identify this?"

Jameson took the canteen and turned it around in his square-fingered hands. He handed it back. "It belongs to one of that rabble what's come in for the army. Where did you get it?"

"Never mind that. Who was this person?"

"Damned if I know. He came for bowls with a bunch of his mates. I made him put it up, just like I make everyone put up their own drink when they bring it with them."

"When, precisely, did he come for bowls, this fellow?"

"The Sunday before last, I should think. It was long ago. I can't be sure."

"You don't remember his name?"

"I don't ask people their names."

"Can you remember what he looked like?"

"Tall, black hair, moustache." Jameson shrugged.

"That's helpful," Gilbert said, although it wasn't very helpful at all. Half the people in this part of England were tall with black hair and moustaches.

"I did notice them playing with that Ormyn fellow," Jameson added.

"Them? The soldiers?"

"Did you think I meant someone else?"

"When?"

"It would have had to be Sunday before last, wouldn't it? Because Ormyn was dead by last Sunday."

"Indeed."

"Ormyn lost quite a bit of money, too, as I recall. There was some shouting about it in the lane. I almost had to send one of the boys out to separate them. And one of Wattepas' journeymen was involved, as well. Wace, I think his name is."

"Wace," Gilbert muttered, struggling to get a grip on the implications of this disclosure.

Jameson leaned close and bellowed in Gilbert's ear, "Wace! That's what I said!"

"I'm not deaf, you know." Gilbert rubbed his ear.

"But you're dumb as a post. I'll never understand why Edith married you, anyway."

"It's because I'm so handsome and charming. Unlike you."

"I won't be insulted in my own house."

"But you feel free to insult your guests? That's hardly fair. Oh, and there's one other thing." Gilbert produced the drawing of Ormyn's sword, which he had forgotten about until this moment. "You wouldn't have any idea what happened to this, would you?"

Jameson batted the picture down. "Get out of my house! I'm done talking with the likes of you!"

Chapter 13

"All right, then, listen up," Parfet said to the thirty-odd men all in their armor assembled in the bailey. "The usual rules apply. No one goes out alone. Keep in pairs or threesomes. All plunder will be put in a common pool, which we will divide up into equal shares when we return. I'll whip anyone who keeps anything to himself. Understand?"

There were nods all around.

"Good," Parfet said. "For those of you who've never done this before, don't worry. Do your jobs well and there will be plenty for all of us. Now, mount up, and let's get going. We've got ten miles or more to cover, and I want to be in position before dark."

The men going on the raid mounted their horses and took up the lead ropes of the pack horses, and began to file out of the gate, Parfet in front, followed by Melmerby and then Stephen. As they passed the remains of the village and headed downhill toward the ford of the Severn, Parfet turned in the stirrups to get a look at the men trailing up the path. "Close it up, there!" he shouted to those who had already allowed gaps to grow between them. "No laggards! Keep together!"

"Shall I go back and give them some encouragement?" Stephen asked.

"No, they'll be fine as long as we keep an eye on them."

The men on picket at the ford waved as the leading horses splashed into the river, which was only up to a man's knees here. On the other side, which was lined with oaks, beech, and willow, there was a broad field that gave the appearance of a sheep run. No one was about, nor any sheep. The path from the ford curved toward the southwest along the river, but the Welsh guide at the head of the party led them westward across the field toward a forested hill a mile or so away. Their route henceforth would be over the hills and away from the paths and the few roads that criss-crossed the region in the valleys, for although the going was slower, they were less likely to startle any of the native Welsh, who could be counted on to give the alarm.

The raiding party reached the hills above the objective, a village called Llanfair or Llanvair, depending on who pronounced the name, half an hour before dark. Parfet, Mably, and Stephen left the men to set up camp while, followed by Melmerby, they went over the crest of the hill and descended the steep slope to the edge of the wood in order to get a look at the village. This spot gave them an excellent view. All Llanfair lay before them in the river valley, fifty or more houses on the south side of the river with a neat little stone church and a fat manor house not far from where a bridge crossed over, more steep hills on the northern side rising from the river bank.

"You couldn't wish for better," Parfet said. "We'll hit them at dawn just as they're waking up."

"It shouldn't take long to strip the place, m'lord," Melmerby said. "We'll be done and on our way back by noon."

"And home before nightfall," Mably said.

"I'd like that," Parfet said. "Away before they can summon help. This will be fun."

Anyone whose knowledge of warfare derived from the ancient sources like Polybius, Livy, and Tacitus might expect a soldier's life to turn around great battles. But he would be wrong. Stephen's experience had taught him that the main work of soldiering was raiding and pillaging, punctuated by the occasional siege, and skirmishing, a lot of skirmishing. In Spain, he had found pillaging to be unexciting work which involved making sure that the men took what was needed and they didn't get drunk or out of hand. Skirmishing was the heady stuff that knights lived for and where reputations were often made, but he hoped this time, as the raiding party filed out of the hills to the road running northward toward the town, that there would be none of that. He still didn't have confidence in Harry's modified stirrup, and wanted to avoid testing it against sharps carried by enemies who meant real harm.

The covered stirrup had provoked some comment, mainly snide remarks from Mably, and sidelong looks from men such as Dogface, whose real name was Perkins, and his friend Gregory (the men had the good sense to keep their contempt among themselves) — and the fact that Stephen had taken to riding with shorter stirrups than customary, a length like that used by the Spanish light horse. He thought he had more stability with this shortened stirrup length, given his infirmity. The longer length required the rider to keep pressure on the stirrup bar using his toes and the ball of the foot, but this was impossible for Stephen, since he had neither toes nor ball on his left foot. He had ridden enough with the *jinetes*, the Spanish light horse, to be familiar with this style of riding, for Spanish knights did not scruple to ride as light horse when the need arose, unlike the English knight, for whom light horse was a subject of derision.

The head of the column reached the road and turned right toward Llanfair. A short distance ahead was a one-horse cart carrying a load of hay toward town. A boy on the back spotted the raiders immediately and shouted an alarm to the driver. Parfet broke into a canter as the driver glanced at them over a shoulder and lashed the horse to dash for the village. A cart horse was no match in a race with a mounted man, and the raiders overtook the cart without difficulty. The driver and the boy abandoned the cart and ran into the neighboring field descending a hill on the left. Parfet kept going and, picking up speed, he rounded a bend where another road came in from the west. Several archers at the back of the column paused to overturn the cart and set it afire. Then they hastened to catch up with the main body.

Shortly after they passed the cart, the head of the column rounded another gentle bend to the left, and there ahead lay the first houses of the village and a third bend brought the tower of the village church into view.

The raiders charged down the road three abreast with Parfet, Melmerby, and Mably in the lead.

What they thought was a manor house turned out to be the home of a wool and cattle merchant. It lay by the foot of a hill behind two houses at the head of Bridge Street, where there was a wide expanse that had to be the town marketplace. A good portion of the raiders crowded into the merchant's yard until Parfet sent them off to start looting the houses along the street and collecting all the livestock they could find, superintended by Mably, while he and Stephen, whose task it seemed was to guard Parfet, climbed the steps to the door, which Melmerby held open for them.

The owner of the house had just risen, for he was partly dressed and throwing on his coat as Parfet and Stephen strode into his hall. The man's wife and what had to be a pair of daughters watched from the top of the stairs.

"What is the meaning of this outrage?" the owner shouted in good English.

"We've come to pay your pleasant town a visit," Parfet said. "Don't look so shocked. We are at war, after all. Your people have done all manner of harm in our lands as it is. This is only justice. If you cooperate, no one will be hurt, which I cannot say was a promise you made to our folk." He motioned to Melmerby. "Take him around the town and have him repeat this to the townsfolk. I don't want them making any trouble."

"Right away, sir," Melmerby said. He grasped the owner by the collar and dragged him from the house.

Parfet gestured toward the stairs. "See what they've got hidden up there."

The soldiers who had followed them into the hall charged up the stairs, while another party invaded the pantry, and others outside attacked the kitchen, barn, pigsty, and chicken coop.

Before long, the possessions of the house were raining into the yard from the upper windows to be collected and piled in the street where all the loot was being gathered. Parfet and the others were especially excited by the find of silver plate in the pantry as well as a hefty money box chained to the corner post of a bed in the master's chamber.

Melmerby returned with the wool merchant whom he released to join his family on the floor above. "M'lord," he said, "the boys have asked me to tell you there's something in the undercroft they think you'd like to see."

"Shall we?" Parfet said to Stephen.

They descended the front stairs and entered the undercroft, where a dozen soldiers were standing around four large barrels. The barrels were taller and narrower than English barrels, and were instantly identifiable as French or Gascon.

Parfet grinned when he saw them. "What do we have here, eh?"

"Looks to be wine, m'lord," one of the soldiers said. "French wine."

"French wine, indeed," Parfet said. "Who would have thought we'd find such a thing in this awful place. Pull the bung on that one so we can be sure." He pointed to one of the barrels.

A soldier pried out the bung. Parfet put his nose to the hole. He straightened upon. "Wine, indeed! First-rate wine, if my nose is any judge!"

"You wouldn't mind if we tried it," a soldier said, "just to be sure it ain't gone bad, would you, m'lord?"

"We'll take it back with us," Parfet said. "Find me a cart."

A cart with a horse was produced in short order and the casks loaded, then wheeled into the street, where a substantial pile had grown as the houses hereabout surrendered their contents — mainly the most valuable and portable stuff like pots and pans and plates of brass, kettles, drinking vessels, the odd silver cup or plate, bolts of linen and wool, and piles of clothing — while just down the road a herd of horses, cattle, and sheep, along with a few pigs, here corralled by a line of archers.

"There's more than we can take back on the pack horses," Mably said to Parfet. "More than I expected."

"It's early yet," Parfet said squinting at the sun, which was concealed by gray clouds and was visible only as a dim glow. "We'll use carts. There's still time to get safely away. See what you can do."

While Parfet and Mably turned their attention to the matter of securing enough carts and getting them loaded, Stephen, whose protection no longer seemed to be needed, wandered back into the wool merchant's yard. Now that the house had been stripped of what could be carried off, the yard was deserted, the front door and the doors to the undercroft standing open.

Stephen heard a woman's voice from one of the upstairs windows. The words were Welsh and beyond his understanding in themselves but the tone pleading. He could think of only one reason why the woman might be pleading, and he dropped his shield and helmet, and bounded up the stairs two at a time. He crossed the hall at a run and clambered up to the second floor. The voice came from the master bed chamber.

The door was ajar. Stephen stepped into the room. The wool merchant, his wife, and youngest daughter, a girl of no more than ten, were crouched by one of the windows, a soldier named Michael standing over them with a drawn dagger in case any of them decided to intervene. The wife was the pleader and she was still at it as Stephen surveyed the rest of the scene. The eldest daughter, a girl of about thirteen or so, had been laid upon the bed. Dogface held down one arm while Greg had the other. The girl's skirts had been thrown up to reveal her legs, which were crossed at the ankles, and her underclothes had been cut off. Her face was resolute as she resisted Melmerby's efforts to pry them apart.

"Oh, yer honor," Melmerby said at the sight of Stephen in the doorway. "Would you like to go first?"

"There's no time for this," Stephen said. "They're loading up now. We'll be going soon."

Melmerby took this to mean that Stephen had rejected his offer. "We won't be long."

"Let me say it more plainly then. Get going."

"Sir Richard won't mind if we have a bit of fun," Melmerby said in a sulky tone.

"I'm not going to repeat myself, Melmerby. Every hand's needed. That includes yours."

Melmerby cursed and got off the bed. Dogface and Greg released the girl's arms. She rolled off the bed and ran out of the chamber without a glance at Stephen.

"Let's go, boys." Melmerby swaggered by Stephen to the door, Greg and Michael at his heels.

Dogface paused and brushed the younger daughter's cheek. She tried to draw away, but the wall behind her prevented it. "She's such a pretty piece. You sure we can't take her with us?"

"No," Stephen said. "You can't."

Dogface went out.

The wife had stopped her bawling, but she did not look grateful. She rose to her feet, her face filled with hate. The woman's expression catapulted Stephen back in time to a house in Spain. His friend Rodrigo's men had found the harem of the petty chieftain whom they had just killed and whose land they had raided, and wanted to rape the women. Rodrigo's standing order was that no rapes should occur, and Stephen had enforced that order with the same vigor with which he carried out all his duties. The women had regarded him with the same hate as the Welsh woman. Except for one, a black-haired beauty with a hooked nose. She had looked relieved. She stood up and crossed from of the tangle of women crouching by a window. "I'm glad you killed him," she said to Stephen as she stood before him.

"What's your name?" he asked, so stunned by her beauty that he could barely speak.

"Taresa is the name he gave me," she replied.

"You belonged to him?"

"I did."

He took her wrist. "You belong to me now."

"If you can keep me," she said. But she had come without compulsion and had remained with him until she died. The ache left by her death was as fresh as if she had gone yesterday. Their son, Christopher, looked like her except for the nose.

Stephen said to the wool merchant, "Get away and stay away until we are gone. Understand?"

The merchant nodded.

Stephen went down to the hall, his coif back, arming cap in his belt, since there was no imminent danger of attack by the townspeople. It was quiet here. He wondered where the older daughter had gone. He hoped she had the sense to hide.

He heard scraping on the floor behind and turned, expecting to see the older daughter slipping from one bolt hole to another.

It was the soldier Michael. His right arm was upraised, a dagger in his fist.

Stephen barely had time to throw out his left arm and intercept the blow, which struck his mailed shoulder rather than his face, the intended target. Stephen pivoted and threw Michael with a hip toss. Michael's momentum carried him over so that he was unable to keep his feet and they struck the ground, Stephen on top. Michael used the remaining momentum to roll Stephen over, and straddled him.

Michael struck with the dagger but missed as Stephen ducked his head to the side. Michael put a hand on Stephen's neck to prevent such a thing from happening again and struck once more. Stephen caught the dagger arm with crossed arms and gripped the blade with one hand to strip the dagger from Michael's grasp, but Michael prevented this by clasping Stephen's wrist.

They struggled together, strength against strength, until it occurred to Michael to put his chest against the pommel and use his weight to drive the point home.

There was a flicker of movement at the corner of Stephen's eye which neither he nor Michael paid attention to. But they were not alone in the hall. Someone struck a great blow that landed on Michael's helmeted head with a solid clunk. Michael rolled off. Stephen climbed to his feet and drew his dagger.

Michael shook his head, then ran from the house.

Stephen turned to see who had saved him.

It was the elder daughter. She still held the log she had used against Michael.

Stephen stepped away in case she decided to use the log again.

"*Diolch*," he said: Thanks, one of the few Welsh words he knew. She did not reply.

He left her with her log, and stumped out of the house, thinking of what he would do to Michael when he caught him.

Chapter 14

When Gilbert turned the corner of Linney Lane and Corve Street, he noted that there were knots of people hurrying north toward the bridge over the River Corve. He paused to consider this, since it was an odd thing for people to do during the middle of the day when they should be working.

He was about to dismiss this oddity from his thoughts when a woman in one of the knots spotted him. She pointed at him and said something, accompanied by a cackle, to one of her companions. Gilbert heard the cackle, though not the commentary, but whatever it was, it provoked smiles on all the faces, which until that moment had held a mixture of expressions ranging from grimness to excited interest.

Gilbert was not a man with a great deal of pride, but like anyone, he did not relish being made fun of, and he had the sensation that the woman had made him the butt of some jape. "Do you see something amusing?" he called to the woman who had spoken.

"What?" she cried back.

"I said, what do you find so amusing?"

"Yer heading in the wrong direction!"

"What are you talking about?"

"You should be going that way!" the woman pointed north toward the bridge.

"Whatever for?"

"Some boys've found a dead man under the bridge!"

Gilbert sighed, abandoning all thought of continuing his investigations today. "Oh, dear," he muttered, as he turned to follow the knots.

There was already quite a crowd on and about the bridge when Gilbert arrived, even though they were out in the country now, away from any of the houses straggling down

Corve Street and along Saint Mary's Lane — far enough in the country that Gilbert wondered how so many had gathered so fast.

As Gilbert came up, the crowd surged around him. One of the men said, "Where's Sir Stephen?"

"He's left town on an errand," Gilbert said. "He won't be coming. Send someone for Sir Geoffrey. You'll find him at the castle."

There was some debate over who should be given this task, since nobody wanted to leave. But eventually a father dispatched one of his sons, who ran off with obvious reluctance.

"Where is he?" Gilbert asked.

"Over here," someone said, and people tugged Gilbert's sleeve, leading him across the bridge to the Smithfield parish side.

"There." One of the men pointed down toward the stream from the foot of the bridge.

Gilbert could just see a pair of legs in the sluggish brown water. The remainder of the body was out of sight among tall grass beneath the bridge.

"Who found him?" Gilbert asked.

"These boys," a man said, indicating a trio of boys about five or six.

Gilbert knelt before the boys. He recognized one of them as living in Lower Galdeford, which was some distance away. "Does your mother know you're here?"

"No," the boy said. "But she don't care."

"I hope you're right, for your sake. Now, tell me, how did you find the body?"

"We was shagging rocks," the boy said. "I thought it was just bit of rubbish and we used him for a target until Milward saw it for what it was."

Milward, the boy next to the speaker, nodded vigorously, as this gave him the credit for the discovery.

"Just a bit of rubbish, eh?" Gilbert mused. "When did this happen?"

"An hour, maybe?" Milward said.

"And you touched nothing?" Gilbert asked.

"Well, we went close, just to be sure," the first boy said. "Then we sent off for Walt's dad." He indicated a smaller boy beyond Milward. "They live close."

"I see," Gilbert said, standing up. He said to the people around him, "Well, then, let's get him out of there and have a look at him."

Several of the men clambered down the bank, and hauled the dead man to the edge of the road. They lay him face down. There was something familiar about him. Gilbert could not put his finger on who it was, although in such a small town it would not be unusual for him to know the victim.

Then one of the men turned the body over.

It was Wace Bursecot, the journeyman goldsmith.

The boy sent to fetch Sir Geoffrey Randall returned without him, and it was a full two hours before the coroner made his appearance on the road from town. By then, people had drifted back to their homes and places of work, since the identity of the victim was now known, so only Gilbert and the jurymen remained, and even the jury wasn't complete, because two of the Smithfield parish men had not turned up. Wace's wife, meanwhile, had come, alerted by neighbors. She had collapsed at the sight of her husband, and the neighbors had carried her home as well, leaving behind the handcart they had brought to take the body back.

A valet accompanying Sir Geoffrey dismounted and stood a folding camp stool near Wace's body. Then he helped Randall slide off his horse. The valet handed a cane to Randall, who hobbled the few steps separating his horse from the stool.

"Your gout bothering you again, sir?" Gilbert asked as Randall settled onto the stool.

"Yes, damn it," Randall snapped. Outbreaks of gout frayed his temper, and this was a bad time to have an attack of the gout, with the army about to march. "Who's this?"

"His name is, or was, Wace Bursecot. He was a journeyman to Leofwine Wattepas."

"The goldsmith?"

"Yes, sir."

"What's he doing here?"

"That's a good question. His wife said he didn't come home last night nor turn up for work this morning, so we think he may have been killed sometime yesterday."

"Humph. Strangled, that much is clear."

"Yes, sir," Gilbert said, for there was a strip of cloth around Wace's neck. It dug so deeply into the flesh that bruising was visible about the cloth. He had seen death like this before, so he had no doubt about this one even without a more thorough examination.

"Anybody see anything?"

"Not as far as we know."

Randall noticed that all the jury wasn't yet present. "Where's Estwyke and Foster?"

"We don't know," Gilbert said.

Randall struggled to his feet. "Well, you know what to do. Get a vote and write it up. I'm going back to the castle. Can't do anything useful here now." He hobbled toward his horse. The valet helped him mount.

"You thinking about doing something with this?" Randall asked Gilbert.

"I don't know, sir."

"Waste of time, chasing after murderers when there's real work to be done. How is Stephen doing with that business of the Prince's, by the way?"

"Hot on the trail, sir."

"Is he? Good. Keep me informed. Whatever happens, have him come to me first so I can take word to the Prince."

"Of course, sir."

"That's a good lad," Randall said. He turned his horse, and he and the valet plodded back toward town.

"It's suppertime," one of the jurymen said. "What are we going to do?"

It was not strictly legal to determine the cause of death without a full jury. But then, it wasn't strictly legal for the coroner to abandon his clerk and the jury to perform their tasks without him. Randall had wanted to be sheriff, but had lost out on that lucrative position, and he had never shown much interest in his job as coroner. He should have established himself in Hereford, the county seat, and personally presided over all the inquests into suspicious deaths in the county. But claiming that his gout made that a hardship, he had instead hired several deputies to perform his duties. None had ever stayed long. Stephen Attebrook was the most capable of the lot, and Gilbert had no expectation that he would last either, given the miserly stipend Randall paid and the sad nature of the work. And that did not take into account Stephen's natural ambition, which would reassert itself once he managed to work himself out of the pit of despair into which the terrible events of Spain had driven him.

"Gilbert?" asked the juryman concerned about supper.

"Sorry, my mind wandered," Gilbert said. "You're right. It's late. We might as well get this over with. Death by foul play, is it?"

There was a quick round of assent.

"That's it, then," Gilbert said. He should have asked them to put a price on the rag used to kill Wace, but the amount would have been so small that it didn't seem worth the effort. "Can someone help me get him into the cart?"

There were no volunteers and Gilbert had to call two of them by name to assist. The body was flaccid and cold, and the skin felt slimy. The three of them lifted the body over the rail and tossed it into the cart, where it landed with a thud. Gilbert was about to ask for help pulling the cart to Wace's house, but the two jurymen, foreseeing this request, said quick good-byes and retreated at a trot across the bridge, leaving

Gilbert alone with the cart and body. The setting sun threw golden light on the bridge, the cart, and the fields about him, but it did nothing to warm his heart.

Gilbert stood between the handrails, looking at poor Wace and contemplating the ordeal ahead. He noticed Wace's hands were wrinkled, like a washerwoman's from long emersion. That was consistent with the notion that someone had strangled him on the bank and then let him fall into the stream. Gilbert wondered if he could have been killed upstream rather than at the bridge, but when he bent over to examine Wace's head, it was clear that there was no evidence of emersion above the shoulders. Gilbert almost turned around and picked up the handrails when he remembered other corpses he and Stephen had examined and been mistaken about because of their haste to reach what had seemed an obvious conclusion.

"I suppose I must," Gilbert sighed. He climbed into the cart and pulled off Wace's coat, shirt, and stockings until Wace lay naked. At least there was no one here but Gilbert and the angels to look at him in this degrading state. Gilbert bent over the body, searching for signs of other injuries than the one on the neck, like a hidden stab wound or a knock on the head. He found nothing of the kind. But there were bruises on both upper arms.

"So," he said, draping a blanket someone had left folded in a corner of the cart over the body, as if he had reached a decisive conclusion, although he had not.

Gilbert hopped down, took up the handrails, and headed back toward town.

He was a hundred yards up the road when he realized that he did not feel the slap of the tin canteen against his hip. He remembered that he had set the canteen on the grass when he had first examined Wace. He wanted to kick himself for forgetting to pick it up again. He left the handcart in the middle of the road and jogged back to the bridge, but when he got there, the canteen was not where he'd left it, nor anywhere about the bridge.

"Oh, dear God!" Gilbert cried. "I've lost it! What will I tell Stephen — or worse, Harry!"

He trudged up the road, the weight of his failure and what that would mean in terms of humiliation and recrimination tugging more heavily upon him than the cart.

Chapter 15

Herbert Jameson waited until the middle of the week, after the army had departed. He should have waited longer, he should in fact have done nothing — that was the prudent thing. But Herbert was not long on prudence any more than his brother. And the thought of how much he might make for the item became too strong to resist.

He had enough animal caution to realize that it was not wise to be seen carrying the item about, nor was it wise to be seen going to his destination, so he waited until dusk to retrieve the item from its hiding place in the thatch of his roof, and then nightfall before he set out.

As his house and his objective both lay outside town, where no curfew officially inhibited nighttime traffic and no bailiffs patrolled, he had little to fear from the law, but Herbert nonetheless was skittish, starting at every sound, as he made his way to Galdeford crossing and down the street through Lower Galdeford. Presently the houses ended and the Augustine priory loomed on the right, and at last, there on the other side of its fence, was Thumper's rambling house, looking like a lumpy hillock in the darkness.

It was early enough yet that people were still up, firelight visible through cracks in the shutters. Herbert knocked on the door. A boy answered, inquired who he was, and disappeared back into the house. A few minutes elapsed, then the door opened again, and Will Thumper stepped back to admit him.

"What can I do for you, Jameson?" Thumper asked. "It's a bit late to be about, isn't it?" Not that Thumper was unused to nocturnal visitors. Owing to the nature of his business, that sort of thing happened quite often.

"I've something to sell," Herbert said. He held out the item.

Thumper unwrapped the cloth surrounding it. He looked closely at the item. "How much you want for it?"

"Five pounds."

"I don't know. I won't be able to get that much when I sell it. I might go a pound."

"Damn it, that's robbery."

"That's rich, coming from you about this. Look, I could get in real trouble if anyone connected me with this thing. I'll have to think about it. Can you come back tomorrow?"

Herbert did not want to come back tomorrow. He wanted this business concluded tonight. But he could see that Thumper would need time to make up his mind. He felt he could depend on Thumper's greed to bring him around, so they would have a deal eventually. "Tomorrow, then."

"Watch yourself on the way back," Thumper said. "The night is full of evil men. We don't want that to be lost."

It was a cold morning and Harry was bundled up against the chill when Broad Gate opened. A couple carts hauling firewood had just passed, and with the street empty, Harry pulled his hood back over his ears so that he saw only the ground in front of him while he worked on another carving of Rosamond. So he did not see who Gip, the gate ward, spoke so sharply to when he said, "Hey, even you got to pay!"

Then Harry heard the reply — "I just need a word with Harry" — and knew who it was.

"What do you need a word with Harry for?" Gip asked.

"Why," there was a chuckle, "we have important business together, Harry and me. I won't be but a moment. You keep an eye on me, if you're worried that I'll bolt into town, but plug your ears. This is secret, like."

The speaker knelt before Harry and put his face close, knowing that no matter what he said to Gip, the ward would do his best to overhear.

"Hello, Will," Harry said, looking up into Will Thumper's face. "What can I do for you?"

"Not much. How's business?" Thumper fingered Harry's cup to get a look inside.

"The usual, now the army's gone, not that that bunch gave much thought to charity."

"Poor fellow. I wouldn't have your life for anything."

"I get the feeling you didn't come for idle chat."

"Well, I am a busy man. Your friend Attebrook, word is he's gone."

"He had an errand that took him to Montgomery. He'll be back shortly."

"I've something he'd like to know."

"What about?"

"There was an item taken from Ormyn, the fellow who died. Attebrook was interested in it."

"So?"

"I know where it is."

"You wouldn't happen to have it yourself, would you?"

"Good God, no. But it was offered to me."

"Ah. By whom?"

"Herbert Jameson."

"Wistwode's nemesis from the Pigeon?"

"I know of only one Herbert Jameson hereabout."

"How did he get it?"

"I don't ask such questions, you know that."

"Attebrook will want to know."

"I'm sure. But he'll have to ask Jameson about it. Say," Thumper gestured at the block of wood in Harry's hands where a face, as yet unidentifiable, was taking shape. "You wouldn't have any more of those carvings of the saint, would you?"

"No, not on hand."

"Have you thought of selling them? Folks are sure to buy them."

"I'd lose my beggar's license if I went into trade. There's not enough money in carving heads to make that worth while."

"Of course. Why do you bother, then?"

"Occupies the mind. It gets boring just sitting here. Talking to Gip is a waste of breath."

"If you make any more, I'll take one for my missus."

"Why don't you see me in a couple of days or three? I'll have something for you then."

Thumper stood up. "Good seeing you, Harry."

"Always a pleasure, Will."

Chapter 16

Stephen rushed through the alley and into the street. Mably, who was superintending the loading of some wagons in the marketplace, heard him coming and turned to see what was up. "What the devil's got into you?" Mably asked, astonished at the sight of Stephen, shield- and helmet-less. Under the circumstances, it was as unusual as if he had appeared hatless or with his bum showing.

"Have you seen that boy, Michael?" Stephen gasped.

"Michael? Michael? I don't know a Michael."

"He must be one of Parfet's people, then. He ran out here only moments ago. From the merchant's house."

"There was someone. I didn't pay much attention. We're quite busy here, you see. Lots to do. More stuff than we ever thought to find in such a small town."

Stephen spotted Parfet and Melmerby outside a tavern at the corner of Bridge and High Streets. Parfet was sipping from a cup, while Melmerby had a pitcher in his hand and was just wiping his mouth from having taken a drink that spilled on his face and spattered his mail. Stephen crossed to them.

"Have you seen Michael?" he asked.

Parfet looked as astonished as Mably had been at the sight of Stephen. "What for?"

"The little bastard just tried to knife me."

"Good God! I don't believe it. Melmerby, do you have any idea what could have got into him?"

Melmerby swirled the contents of the pitcher. Parfet held out the cup. Melmerby filled it. "Well, m'lord, we was about to have a bit of fun with one of the girls there." He gestured toward the wool merchant's house. "Sir Stephen interrupted us. Sent us packing. You were a bit rude about it, too, if you don't mind my saying, your honor. We was having a celebration, like. It was to be Mike's first time. He's a young fellow, you know. Hasn't had any yet." He sighed. "She was a pretty piece, young and a virgin, I'm sure." He smiled apologetically. "It was to be a virgin with a virgin. We thought that appropriate for the occasion."

"I told you there was to be none of that," Parfet said.

"I know, m'lord, but in the excitement we forgot ourselves."

"It's hard to think that Mike would do something like that just because he didn't get laid," Parfet said.

"Well, he is a bit of a hothead, you know, m'lord. I expect he was angry and disappointed."

"That's no reason to go knifing people."

"You know it's happened over less, m'lord."

Parfet harrumphed and drained his cup. "Yes, I suppose it has. It's a crazy world. Go find him. He'll have to pay for this."

"Right, sir." Melmerby handed Stephen the pitcher and turned away.

"I'm sorry this happened," Parfet to Stephen. "I say, what have you done with your shield and helmet? We'll be going soon. Don't want to leave them behind."

Michael could not be found, however. Melmerby brought word that he had last been seen riding west up High Street away from town.

"You can't be serious," Parfet said. "He's fled? Left us?"

"I'm afraid so, sir," Melmerby said.

"In the middle of this wild country," Parfet marveled. "It will be a miracle if he gets back in one piece."

"If he comes back," Melmerby said. "I have the feeling we won't be seeing him again."

"No?"

"I'm sure he's afraid of your wrath, m'lord. You do have a temper."

"Well, he was facing the lash. That would have made amends, wouldn't it, Stephen? I don't like hanging a man when I don't have to."

"I suppose it would," Stephen said.

"And I'll give you Michael's share. How about that?"

Stephen nodded. A part of him would have preferred a hanging, but another part was satisfied with the prospect of a whipping and Michael's share. Some men wore their grudges, even those for minor offenses, like badges. Stephen wasn't without his grudges, but they had been earned by hard, repeated misuse. He didn't stew over outbursts of temper like this.

"Good, then." Parfet surveyed the marketplace, which was now crowded with wagons and the horses of the men. It was nearly noon. "Look's like everyone's ready. Mount up."

"Mount up, everyone!" Melmerby shouted, conveying the command. "Time to go!"

Owing to the wagons and the livestock, they took the east road out of Llanfair. This was the direct route back, if you could call the winding roads of Wales a direct route to anything, but it was the shortest without having to go cross-country, and Parfet reckoned the quickest.

Parfet sent Stephen with two of the men-at-arms ahead of the column about two-hundred yards to serve as an advance party. Their job was to spy out a possible ambush, but the raiding party had moved so soon that no one expected trouble, and they encountered none during the two hours it took to cover the five or so miles to the next village. Stephen paused here at the small church that sat by the road to wait for the guide to come up, for there were two roads out of the village, and he wasn't sure which to take.

"That way," the guide said when he arrived, indicating the south road.

"What's the name of this place?" Stephen asked as they left it.

"Some people call it Dolarthin, others Castle Caereinion," the guide said.

161

"Castle? I didn't see any castle," Stephen said with some alarm, because talk of a castle meant a garrison, which would not be friendly in this country.

"It was back by the church. You saw the mound there, didn't you? That was the motte."

"Yes." Stephen remembered it, little more than an odd hump of ground covered with grass.

"It was burnt long ago."

"That's a relief, I suppose."

"Yes," the guide said, squinting toward the northeast. "I suppose it is. But there's another at Welshpool and that's only five miles off. I would feel better if we were moving faster." He wheeled his horse and returned to the column while Stephen and the men-at-arms trotted ahead to see what the road held in store for them.

Another hour and a half through rolling country that afforded views for miles on the hilltops brought the column to a village where the road crossed a small river. The village was deserted, not a soul in sight on the roads and paths or in the fields around it.

The spring melt had swollen the river to the limits of its banks and crossing would have been difficult had there not been a bridge. However, planks had been removed from the middle of the bridge, making it impassable to wagons and livestock.

"They knew we were coming," Parfet said to Mably and Stephen as they surveyed the damage.

"We'll have to replace them," Mably said. "We should be able to use timbers from one of these houses."

"Right," Parfet said. "Melmerby, have the boys get some boards to cover that gap. Be quick about it. I don't care if you have to pull down houses to get them."

"Right away, sir," Melmerby said, and shouted to some of the archers to get busy.

Although the archers pulled down a wall of the house nearest the bridge, timbers from that house did not prove necessary to mend the bridge, for some of the men who took the opportunity to search nearby houses for whatever the inhabits had failed to carry away found the missing bridge planks behind a privy.

The delay cost half an hour, and it was midafternoon as the column pressed on to the southeast.

A mile outside of the village at the river, the road turned sharply south on flat ground at another village of half dozen houses.

"Richard," Stephen said to Parfet as they turned the corner. "I've a bad feeling."

"About what?" Parfet asked, although from his grim expression it looked as though he shared Stephen's thoughts.

"Welshpool, there's a castle at Welshpool. It's just up the road from where we crossed that river."

"What makes you think so?"

"That's what the guide told me."

"So?"

"I'm afraid the people at the bridge took up the planks and then sent word to the castle. They meant to slow us down so the garrison could catch us."

Parfet locked eyes with Stephen. He was silent for a moment. "You could be right."

"Which means they're on the road behind us and riding like the devil to overtake us. How much farther to the ford?"

"Another mile or so. What are you thinking?"

"A rear guard action to allow the baggage to get across."

"It might work. No harm in being prepared. Melmerby!"

"Yessir!" Melmerby replied.

"Get these people moving! We've only a mile to go, and I want them at a dead run, if they can manage it."

"We're likely to loose much of the livestock."

"But we'll save what's in the wagons and on the pack horses. Sergeants! With me!"

The wagons and pack horses shot ahead at a trot, if not at a dead run, while three of the archers did their best to hurry the cattle and sheep along, using their bows as prods. The remaining knights and men-at-arms — numbering fourteen without Melmerby — followed in a column of twos, Parfet and Mably in the lead, with Stephen bringing up the rear, twisting in the saddle to keep watch behind them.

Parfet had just reached a bend in the road, where a pond stood to the left behind a screen of trees, when Stephen saw the pursuit.

"They're coming!" Stephen shouted.

Parfet reined up and looked back. A column of Welsh men-at-arms was approaching at a fast trot in the distance. Parfet waved his arms. "Form a line! Form a line!"

The men on the road turned into the field and there was much jostling and backing until a short line formed stretching from the marshy ground on the east into a field on the left.

The Welsh column stopped at the sight of the English, then began deploying into a line of their own about two-hundred yards away. They were a formidable sight: Stephen counted at least forty lances, well more than their number.

As Parfet came up beside him, Stephen said, his voice snapping with the tones of command: "Take half the men a hundred yards up the road and reform. I'll follow with the rest when you are set."

Parfet blinked at being commanded so sharply, but he did not argue. Tapping one of the men in the middle of the line, he shouted, "You on the left, follow me!"

He and the others wheeled and raced down the road.

"What was the point of that?" Mably asked, as Stephen kept an anxious eye on the Welsh.

"We can't beat them. We can only hope to slow them down to buy time for the wagons. If they charge now, they'll be disordered. They won't want that, I think. I wouldn't. Softens the blow." He saw that Parfet was reforming behind them. "Let's go."

The place Parfet had selected to reform was upon the road and into a field on the left, where copses of trees grew on either side of the road. Stephen approved of it, since the trees would break up any Welsh charge.

The Welsh apparently realized the unfavorability of the ground, for they came back into column on the road, while Stephen had the people with him take up a position athwart the road between the copses ahead of Parfet's line. The Welsh column stopped. A party cut into the field intending to come around the copse and attack the English flank while the main body probably intended to charge in column up the road. Stephen waved at Parfet. "Fall back again!"

Parfet led his party to a spot just beyond some hedges which lined the road and ran into the fields on either side. As those men scrambled to reform a line, Stephen gave the signal for his party to retreat to them. They galloped down the road just as the Welsh flanking party came around the copse to the left. The flanking party dashed almost alongside Stephen and the men with him as if they were in a race to reach the end of the field, but in the end, the hedges sheltering Parfet brought them to a halt. The Welsh column came up at a more deliberate pace, the commander clearly seeing that the ground remained unfavorable, even with their superior numbers.

"Melmerby should have reached the ford by now!" Parfet cried as Stephen and the men with him reined up and wheeled about to form up. "Should we break for it?"

"They'll be stacked up to cross!" Stephen called back. "We need to buy more time!"

"One more time, then!" Parfet said. "Back again, boys!"

Parfet's company raced down the road again, while Stephen eyed the Welsh to the left uneasily, for they were hacking a way through the hedge with their swords. It wouldn't be long before they forced a passage and were behind him. But what had him more worried was the column on the road, for those Welsh picked up a canter and pounded down the road toward him with what appeared to be an intention to bowl their way through his thin screen.

"I don't think we can hold them here!" Stephen shouted to the men. "Back to Parfet!"

They wheeled about just as the first of the Welsh at the hedge vaulted through the gap they had created.

It was now another race to reach Parfet and whatever temporary safety their numbers afforded.

Parfet had gone more than a hundred yards this time and had disappeared around a bend in the road to the right. Stephen saw him forming up at the crossroads to the ford where more hedges confined the space available to fight as Stephen's men rounded that bend at a dead gallop. Stephen swiveled for a look back to at the column, which was galloping in pursuit.

Stephen and his party passed through Parfet's line, which closed up.

"Lances down!" Parfet shouted. "Charge!"

It seemed a foolhardy order for so few to charge so many, but Stephen realized it might be the best thing to do in this confined space: throw the enemy into confusion and take out as many as possible before the weight of their numbers could make a difference.

At the last moment, the oncoming Welsh slowed to a trot, since horses could not be made to collide with a wall of spears, and the fight instantly degenerated into a scrum of the push of lances, and when those became useless in the press, of swords and axes. In a flash, the road was a maelstrom of horses stamping and wheeling, and men hacking and stabbing, the only sounds the thump of hooves, the grunting of the combatants, and the thwack of weapons upon shields. There was so little space upon the road that Stephen and his men could only watch for a few moments, until a Welshmen here and there broke through to turn upon the English. Then a party of Welsh came across one of the hedges behind the English, threatening to cut off those in the battle.

Stephen had hoped that his party could serve as a reserve to which Parfet's men might fall back on when they had done enough damage to the Welsh to hold them up for a little while longer. But with the appearance of the flanking party, he realized that could not be. There was only one thing to do now. Honor required it.

"At them, boys!" Stephen shouted, spurring his horse forward.

Before battle there is always anxiety and doubt, but when the lances come down, the horses surge forward, and the impact of the first thrust travels up the lance pole and slams the butt into the armpit, there is a strange joy. It is inexplicable to those who have not experienced it. It is not so much a love of fighting, although there is certainly some of that: the satisfaction of blows well delivered and well turned, of a horse well managed in the confusion, of not running away when a path was clear. It is more the sensation of being surrounded by your friends, all in great danger, each being willing to give his life for his fellows. And although Stephen was a visitor to this company, that special joy came back to him as he took the first Welsh horseman in the back with such an impact that it threw the man to the ground. For a moment, he was in Spain again with Rodrigo, Taresa still lived, and all was right in the world.

After that, as he slipped among the Welsh and they surrounded him, there was the sense that he was outside himself, almost, watching, while some inner power directed his arm as he laid about with his sword or deflected a blow, turning the stallion sometimes with his legs, sometimes with the pressure of his shield on the horse's neck, sometimes with the reins; feeling his sword slam home on a helmet, shoulder, or arm; sensing the enemy's blows thumping on his shield, occasionally glancing off his helmet, other times striking his arms and body; but his mail held, though he would be sorely bruised afterwards.

Here and there men were pulled from their horses or struck down, some of them trampled, others merely stunned or wounded curling into balls hoping for the best, yet others scuttling on hands and knees for the hedges and what safety they afforded.

How long the maelstrom went on and who was winning was always impossible to tell. It often seemed hours but was usually only minutes.

After a time there were no more Welsh about Stephen or the others of his company, and the enemies drew back from each other a spear length, disordered and confused in the narrow expanse of the lane. The English had held; against all expectations, they had held.

Then the pressure of the men in the rear ranks of the Welsh propelled the foremost ahead to the attack again. But this time, the English turned and fled down the road. Everyone knew that in the end it was hopeless and that they had done what they could to protect the wagons, so now their only thought was to get away. No one wanted to die for nothing.

It became a race with the highest of stakes, for the losers on the English side could not expect mercy.

Stephen's stallion was fit and fast, and loved to run. So when Stephen gave the horse his head, it surged ahead of everyone without seeming to exert great effort. It would have been a easy thing to run straight for the ford, but when Stephen cleared the pack, he looked back to see what the Welsh were doing — following hell bent, of course — and what was happening to the others of his company. The English were scattered, some on the road, some having taken to the fields on either side as the hedges broke up and allowed entrance, the slower ones among them already being caught by the fastest of the Welsh.

The road dipped through a small stream. The stallion leaped the stream without being asked, and came down hard on the other side. Stephen absorbed the jolt with his heels, and glanced back again. To the left, three English leaped the stream, pursued by at least ten of the Welsh, pelting over the turf, the hooves of the horses throwing up great clods of grass and dirt, manes and tails flying.

The Welsh were almost upon those three English and it would take only seconds before they were caught and brought down. Stephen swerved into the field and angled toward them. Just as one of the Welsh caught one of the English — Stephen recognized Dogface, his expression panic stricken as he watched his death approach — Stephen brought his stallion shoulder to shoulder with the Welsh horseman and stabbed the man over his shield. The point of Stephen's sword snagged in the mail aventail at the Welshman's throat, but the force of the blow drove him out of the saddle, the now riderless horse galloping on with the others.

"Faster!" Stephen shouted to Dogface.

"He's going as fast as he'll go!" Dogface replied, so bent over the pommel of his saddle that he seemed to be lying atop his mount.

A hedge stood in their way, the boundary to a field, an obstacle those in flight had not taken into account when they picked this route. Two of the English swerved farther left to avoid it, drawing off half the pursuers, but Stephen and Dogface drove straight for the hedge. Stephen felt the stallion hesitate, not liking the sight of that hedge, but Stephen gouged hard with his spurs to keep the horse going, only at the last two strides sitting back deep in the saddle, collecting the stallion to slow him down and to put his weight on the hindquarters, yet still urging him into the jump.

The stallion reared and sailed over the hedge, his hooves brushing the topmost branches, which a proper reeve should have trimmed.

Stephen looked back again. Dogface also had cleared the hedge, as had five of the Welsh on their tail. The horse of a sixth had refused the jump and thrown its rider into the hedge.

It was a clear meadow ahead to the ford, no more than a quarter mile. Two wagons were halted at the ford waiting to cross, while to the right along the track, the livestock was scattering at the approach of the horsemen. Their archer attendants could be seen riding hard for the ford, wanting nothing to do with the Welsh, their only thought to get away.

Stephen let the stallion extend, feeling the easy, powerful stride and the wind in his face almost with pleasure. There were fewer things more satisfying than riding a horse at a dead run across an open field, and he would have enjoyed it more had it not been for the Welsh.

He and Dogface sped by an astonished boy with the staff of a shepherd, although his flock had abandoned him, fleeing from the commotion to the far reaches of the meadow.

Stephen swiveled back for another look at the pursuit. His stallion was faster than any of the others and he was drawing away. But the Welsh were closing on Dogface again, whose horse was not so fine as either he or the enemy possessed. They might catch Dogface before he reached the ford, if Stephen as any judge. He checked up the stallion until Dogface was at his side and then gave the stallion his head, but held back enough to keep pace with Dogface.

The Welsh were close enough that Stephen could see their faces. One called out in good English, "Stand and fight, you coward!"

"I don't like the odds!" Stephen replied.

"You yellow shit!"

"Fuck you and your mother!"

"That's telling 'em, sir," Dogface said. "But what are we going to do?"

"Well, one thing we can do is get more speed out of that nag you're riding." Stephen leaned over and swatted Dogface's horse on the flank with the flat of his sword, and it leaped ahead.

"You could at least have warned me!" Dogface cried, holding onto the mane.

They reached the wagons just ahead of the Welsh. Stephen came round to put the wagons between him and the enemy, and reined up. It was unsafe to drive the horse into the ford. The bed of the river here was made up of large round stones, the ones projecting above the water green with moss. Any horse had to be taken across slowly so as not to break a leg. Dogface was less mindful of this danger and rode into the ford. The horse slipped on a stone and fell on its side, pitching Dogface into the water, then clambered to its feet and walked to the other side.

Stephen dismounted and pushed the stallion into the ford. "Take him!" he ordered Dogface who was climbing to his feet, shaking his head at the fall.

Then he turned to face the Welsh alone.

"I'll fight the one with the big mouth man-to-man, if he has the stomach for it," Stephen said to them.

The Welsh riders regarded him with leveled lances. Just when Stephen thought that they might charge, their eyes flicked to the opposite bank. Five archers had come out on the stony bar with nocked arrows. One of the men-at-arms said something in Welsh to the others. They raised their lances and turned away, leaving three with the wagons while the remainder headed back up the track, where Stephen could see that the English had been surrounded.

Chapter 17

Stephen crossed the ford to the opposite bank and the archers. "Thanks. That was a close one."

"Do you think they'll come back and attack us?" one of the archers asked.

Stephen squinted through the trees to the spot where the Welsh had caught up with Parfet and Mably. The battle was over and the Welsh could be seen stripping the dead. It did not look as though anyone had survived. "I doubt it. They probably don't know how few've been left at the castle. They'll be afraid of a sortie and being caught on this side of the river."

"That's a relief."

"I suppose it is. Come on. We can't do anything useful here."

The pack train and three of the wagons had made it across the river, and Stephen and the archers caught up with them at the gate to the fortress. With Mably and Parfet apparently dead, he was the senior person at Old Montgomery now and the men standing about the bailey with somber faces looked at him as if asking what should be done next. Stephen ordered them to unload the wagons and pack horses. While they did so, he rode alone to the ford so see for himself what the Welsh might be up to. But by the time he returned, the wagons on the other side of the river were gone, and so were the Welsh men-at-arms. The meadow was quiet, as though nothing untoward had happened. It was just another spring day.

When Stephen returned to the castle, he led the wagons back to the ford and across it. None of the men of the garrison were eager to come, but he had ordered them in rather harsh tones that they must recover the bodies of the fallen.

The dead lay upon the road leading from the ford where they had made their stand. They had been stripped of their armor and weapons, but at least the Welsh had the decency to leave them clothed, although the bodies were barefoot since the boots of the dead had been taken as well.

Melmerby ran into the circle of bodies, and found Parfet lying upon his back, staring at the sky with the single eye that remained to him; the left one had been destroyed by what appeared to be the blow of an axe. Parfet's face was marred by other terrible wounds to his face and neck as well. It looked as though he had been hacked repeatedly while he lay on the ground. Melmerby placed his hand on Parfet's chest.

Dogface patted Melmerby's shoulder. "Come away there, lad. We'll take care of him."

"I can't believe he's gone," Melmerby sobbed, as he rose and let Dogface lead him to the wagons.

"You know you had to part from him, the way things are. Sooner rather than later, too."

"Shut up, you ass." Melmerby shook his head and dropped his face into his hands.

Stephen superintended the grim business of loading the bodies onto the wagons — but not those of Mably and Parfet. Theirs were draped across the backs of horses. As undignified as that was, it was better than being in the pile of the other dead.

What had been the chapel was partly roofless. This did not seem a place to leave the dead until they could be buried, so Stephen directed that the bodies be put in the barn overnight, where they lay next to the plunder they had died to protect. Before the door closed upon them, Stephen paused for a last look. He wondered if his choice of tactics had led to this, if he had let Parfet guide the battle whether it could have been avoided, if the survivors blamed him for the disaster. He could not help but think that he was at least partly at fault and that others would reach the same conclusion.

The following morning Stephen rode down to New Montgomery to fetch a priest and to tell the castle commander what had happened.

The commander, Hugh de Tuberville, was a lean, craggy man. He looked Stephen over when he presented himself in the hall. "Who are you?"

"I am Stephen Attebrook. I am a deputy coroner of Hertfordshire."

"What the devil are you doing here?"

"I was sent by the Prince to make an inquiry of Richard Parfet."

"That doesn't explain what you're doing *here*."

"Sir?"

"Here! It doesn't explain what you're doing in my hall."

"I've come to report a mishap."

"What sort of mishap? A murder? We're a bit outside of your jurisdiction."

"No, sir. This is a military matter."

"What could you have to do with a military matter?"

So Stephen told him.

Tuberville listened with a grim face to Stephen's report of the disaster. "Caught on the way back, were you?"

"In sight of the ford, my lord," Stephen said.

"Slowed down because of the wagons," Tuberville snorted. "You idiots. What made you think that with Welshpool so close that you'd get away?"

"Parfet thought we could."

"Parfet! I sent him up to watch the ford. That's all he was fit to do. He wasn't a soldier. He could barely tell one end of a sword from another. And you, what were you doing on this stupid expedition? Thinking to make a quick and easy profit, where you?"

Stephen hesitated, then nodded. "Yessir. I'm afraid so."

Tuberville stroked his chin. "Fifteen men to forty, eh? You held them off long enough for most of the wagons to cross?"

"Three of the five, my lord. We lost all the livestock."

"Not a total loss, then. Although how I'm to replace the men, I've no idea. And I need all I can get." Tuberville called to a servant. "Howard! Have a horse saddled for me! I've got to run up to Old Montgomery to see what sort of mess those young hotheads have made of things!"

The grave was not yet finished by the time Stephen, Tuberville and his escort, and the parish priest reached Old Montgomery, as only two shovels could be found. There was no consecrated ground within the bailey, of course, so the dead were to be buried in what had been the yard of the village church. It would be a single grave for all eleven of the dead, including Parfet and Mably, one long and rather shallow ditch.

Tuberville inspected the bodies without bothering to dismount, and turned away with a curt, "Come along," to Stephen, leaving the priest to do his somber work.

"Show me what you got," Tuberville said as they rode through the gate to the bailey.

"This way, sir," Stephen said. "I've had it put in the barn."

While Tuberville inspected the plunder, Stephen mustered what remained of the garrison for inspection. All the fifteen archers who had gone on the raid survived, and with the six left behind that reduced the complement to twenty-one, plus Melmerby, Dogface, and Greg, who had split from the group about Parfet before it was surrounded.

Tuberville came out of the barn and stood before the assembly. It was clear from his expression that he was angry. "Pathetic," he pronounced. "God help you all if the Welsh come. This place won't hold for half an hour. But it must be held nonetheless. So you will have to remain. Don't any of you do anything so stupid as to cross the river again." He faced Stephen. "Have the goods taken to New Montgomery straightaway."

"My lord," Stephen said quietly so that only Tuberville could hear, "it would be unfair not to share out some of it with them. They took the risks their officers asked of them, after all."

Tuberville bit his lip. Stephen expected a sharp retort. Tuberville asked, "You aren't expecting a share, are you?"

"No, sir. Not now."

Tuberville nodded. "All right then." He said loudly enough for the rest to hear, "I'll have an accounting done, and we'll pay you a piece of it. Now get back to work. And I want you out of here by dawn tomorrow, Attebrook."

After supper as it grew dark, the servants stacked the tables against a wall and threw more wood on the hearth. The center of the hall grew warm and those not on watch clustered about the fire. Melmerby came up behind Stephen as he finished a cup of cider.

"Why don't you try some of this?" Melmerby asked holding forth a brass pitcher. "It's a bit stronger than that piss they served at supper."

"What is it?"

"Let me have your cup." Melmerby poured from the pitcher. "Dogface sends this with his compliments for your help yesterday during the retreat."

Stephen knew it was wine rather than ale from the smell alone. "Where did you get that?"

"It fell off the wagon. Sort of, anyway."

"How much fell off?"

"There might have been a pitcher or two lost. You won't let on when you get to New Montgomery tomorrow, will you?"

"I have no intention of stopping at the castle."

"Good, sir. Oh, and there's that matter of your bowling debt. How were you planning to pay it off?"

Stephen had forgotten about that. He had no money to speak of, only a few pence to cover his traveling costs, and that was not nearly enough to satisfy his debt. "I don't have any money. But you can have my helm. Will that do it?"

"It would indeed, sir. A very fine piece of work it is. Thank you. Thank you so much. Don't bother getting up. We'll settle up in the morning before you leave." Melmerby drank from the pitcher and retreated into a dark corner of the hall.

One of the servants shook Stephen awake at dawn. "Time to get up, sir. I've sent one of the grooms to ready your horses. Cook will have some bread and cheese for you to take with you in short order."

"Thank you, Egbert, I appreciate it."

Stephen rose and struggled into his gambeson. Those going on watch were already up and just leaving, two of their number taking the rear door leading to the motte in order to climb to the tower. A watch was kept in the tower only during the day.

Stephen was finishing the ties on his mail when one of the men sent to the tower returned. "Sir," the soldier said, "could you come? There's been an accident."

"What sort of accident?"

"It's Melmerby, sir. He's dead."

The door to the tower stood open and Stephen could see the body as he strode across from the ramp leading to the top of the motte. The other watchmen stood over the body.

Stephen paused in the doorway to get a sense of things. This tower was like so many others of its kind in that it resembled the belfry of a church, the massive supports at the corners and thus the walls leaning slightly inward so that each floor diminished in size the higher it was. Unlike some towers, though, this one was open clear to the top floor, with walkways at each stage rather than proper floors. A series of ladders gave access upward.

Melmerby lay on his back, arms splayed, one eye half open. A dark stain covered one shoulder. Stephen knelt and fingered the stain. It was still damp. He leaned over to sniff it: wine. He noticed the brass pitcher on its side not far away from the body. There had been enough wine in that pitcher for a man to get very drunk. Stephen imagined him climbing the tower ladders in the dark. A drunk could easily lose his footing in such a place. He wondered what Melmerby had been doing here. No one went to towers after dark . . . unless they had business they wanted to transact out of sight and sound of everyone else. It occurred to him that drinking up stolen wine might provide sufficient reason.

"It's said you're a coroner. You must be familiar with such things. Do you think he fell, sir?" asked the watchman who had fetched Stephen. He had been on the raid, but Stephen could not remember his name.

"It looks that way." Part of Stephen felt compelled to inquire further. Something seemed wrong about this, yet he had no idea what it was: just a nagging sense. But he reminded himself that this sort of thing was no longer his business. He was done with coroner work. He had awaked during the night with the solution to his money problem. He had heard Harry's voice in his head telling him to sell his two mares. Harry had often given him this advice in life and Stephen had just as often refused it. He had so little left after the disasters in Spain that he could not bear to part with a bit of it, for he could not face sinking any lower in the world than he already had. But now his situation was desperate, and the mares were the only property he could sensibly part with; together they might bring as much as fifteen pounds. That was more than enough to buy a passage to France and to provide something to live on while he found another position. So he had decided at last and with great reluctance to take Harry's advice. With Harry's modified stirrup, he could ride in battle with anyone. He'd be safe from the Prince and FitzAllen and there was hope for the future.

Stephen said, "I'll tell the deputy coroner on my way through New Montgomery. Meanwhile, you two stay with the body until he shows up. See that nothing is disturbed."

Chapter 18

Jennifer Wistwode brought out Harry's supper that evening. She set the platter on the bench by his head. Harry smelled bacon, cheese, and mutton porridge. He could see that the porridge had radishes and peas floating with bits of real mutton in its gelatinous deliciousness. He forced himself not to snatch the platter and to attack the food, for Jennie did something quite unusual. Instead of retreating to the house, she sat on the bench by the platter. This caused Harry to be torn by his desire for the food and his wish to savor her presence.

She watched the house, where several of the hall's windows were open. Movement could be seen inside, and it was clear she was watching in case her mother saw her.

Harry carefully put the platter in his lap. "Thanks, Jen."

Jennie leaned over and brushed his chin. "You need another shave, Harry."

"Shaves cost money," he said, going still until Jennie withdrew her hand. The smell of her was almost overwhelming: a mixture of lavender and other scents he could not identify, as the use of scents was not common among the women of his acquaintance, except the whores he occasionally saw at the Wobbly Kettle, and he had never asked them.

"You can afford it now."

Harry sighed as he tucked into his supper. "Business at the gate has been bad since I've cleaned up. People aren't as charitable as they used to be."

"I don't know why. You still look pathetic."

"Thanks. Pathetic is the look I've always aspired to ever since I was a boy."

"Have you got anything more for me?"

"I've one that's half done. Why?"

"There's a fellow at the inn. He asked after a carving. But he's leaving in the morning."

"I could finish it tonight, I suppose. I'll need a candle, though. The one I've got won't last longer than it takes to piss."

Jennie's face screwed up in thought. She took after her parents, round in face and stout in body, yet the expression made her look adorable to Harry. She said, "Can't let you have a candle in there. So much hay."

"I'll be careful. I ain't burned the place down yet."

"I don't know."

"Put it in one of the lanterns, then. It ought to be safe there."

"All right. It'll have to be after dark, though. Mum will wonder what I'm doing with a lantern while it's still light." She stood up.

"Can't have your mum wondering what you're doing." Harry wished she could linger a while longer, but he could not think of anything to say that would persuade her to do so. "Oh, can you ask your father to come out? I've learned something that I think he'd like to hear."

Harry took out the half-finished carving and was working on it while some light remained when Gilbert emerged from the house. He stashed the carving under his cloak as Gilbert crossed the yard.

"Jennie said you've some gossip for me," Gilbert said, settling on the bench.

"I take offense at that. I do not deal in gossip. This is an important matter."

"You are the worst gossip-monger I know, apart from Mistress Bartelot, that is."

"I am cut to the quick that you should compare me with her."

"Out with it. It's getting late."

"Yes, you're such a busy man, filling every minute of daylight with important work. Can't spare a second to talk to the likes of me."

"I like to avoid unpleasantness, if I can."

"Life is full of unpleasantness. You come to me to get used to it. I harden you to life's adversities."

Gilbert stood up. "I've had enough. I'd like to enjoy my evening."

Harry grasped the hem of Gilbert's shirt. "Will Thumper came to see me today."

Gilbert sat down again. "Why would Thumper do that?"

"He had something he wanted Stephen to know. Since Stephen isn't here, I thought you should hear of it."

"That was thoughtful — so unlike you, Harry."

"Seeing as you bollixed up your inquiry by losing that valuable piece of evidence, it occurred to me this was an opportunity to redeem yourself."

"What did Thumper have to say?"

"I think I am entitled to a 'thank you.'"

"That will come if your news is worthwhile."

"Everything thing I say is worthwhile. You're just too dull-witted to appreciate it."

"If it is your intent to make fun of me, I shall go."

"You're such an easy target. But wait! He said . . . ."

Gilbert was quiet for several minutes. At last he said, "Well, this opens up a whole new line of inquiry."

"That's stating the obvious. You may not yet find the relic, but you now have the opportunity to cover yourself with glory by solving the riddle of Ormyn's death. Not that anyone cares."

"But I shall be able to console myself with some success, eh?"

"I don't want you to regard your life as an utter failure."

Gilbert patted Harry' head. The gesture was so quick that Harry, who took offense at being patted on the head, could neither duck nor bat the offending hand away. "Good boy, Harry."

"Where's my thank you?"

"That was it, in case you missed it."

"That's the last favor I do for you."

"No, it isn't. You relish being the center of attention too much to keep your mouth shut next time some insignificant bit of news comes your way."

"You are an insufferable little man."

"But at least I am taller than you."

"Now. It didn't use to be that way."

"No, sadly it didn't. You were tall once, and strapping. I remember how you used to come and cut our wood." Gilbert gazed into the distance, recalling the memory. "Now if you will excuse me, I have a few things to do before bed."

Constables of castles, particularly those who double as deputy sheriffs, are busy men, and so it was well into the morning of the following day before Gilbert succeeded in obtaining an audience with Walter Henle.

When Gilbert at last was allowed to come to the high table in the hall, where Henle was holding court, he received a scowl of dislike that was so intense that it might have shriveled other men. In previous times, before the coming of Stephen Attebrook, they had got on well enough, which is to say that Henle found Gilbert beneath his notice. But an incident involving an interrupted hanging, in which Stephen had played a part, caused Henle to put Gilbert in the category of persons he actively hated.

"What is it?" Henle said at the sight of Gilbert standing there, floppy hat being wrung by stubby fingers. He sounded much put upon.

"May I have a word, your honor — in private?"

"You can say what you have to say right here. I've much to do and very little time, and I don't want to waste it on you."

"It is a rather sensitive matter, your honor."

"Come on, speak out. Get it over with."

As it was clear that Henle would not adjourn to a side chamber, Gilbert leaned across the table so that he would not have to speak loudly in order that what he had to say would not be overheard, and perhaps acted upon. But Henle growled, "Stand up straight, man!"

"Of course, your honor," Gilbert said, standing up straight, his fingers working his hat with more vigor than before. "It is about the matter of Ormyn Yarker."

"Yarker? That fellow who fell off the wall?"

"There is some reason to believe that he did not fall."

Henle started to say something, reconsidered and then said, "You cannot be suggesting that he had help."

"It may be so."

"And who thinks so? You and that good-for-nothing Attebrook?"

"The facts as we know them seem to point in that direction."

"And I suppose there's something you want me to do."

"I need to have some persons arrested. For questioning. And a house searched."

"And who would this be?"

So Gilbert told him.

Henle was too august a person to dirty his hands with little things like arrests and house searches. He delegated that chore to Turling, who summoned six men and went straight away to Linney Gate and downhill to the Pigeon Inn. Gilbert waddled in their wake to keep up as best he could, as they walked even faster than Stephen normally did in their haste to reach the inn before word of their mission got there first.

Gilbert remained in the yard while Turling and the others entered the inn. He was rather interested to see the inside of the house, mainly as a matter of professional innkeeper curiosity, since he had never seen more than the kitchen and the hall. But he deemed it inappropriate under the circumstances to indulge that impulse. Occasionally, he heard angry voices inside, often Herbert Jameson's complaining about some bit of damage, and quite a bit of banging around.

At last, Turling and the other soldiers emerged with Herbert Jameson in hand. Turling carried a sword with a distinctive U-shaped cross and tear-shaped pommel.

"You found it," Gilbert said to Turling with relief. He had been afraid that it would be gone.

Turling nodded, looking angry. The other soldiers were angry as well.

"You!" Jameson said as he realized Gilbert was part of this invasion. "You're behind this! You planted that in my house!" He pointed to the sword. "You've wanted to put me out of business for years!"

One of the soldiers cuffed Jameson so hard that he stumbled and fell to his hands and knees. The soldier added a kick to the ribs that knocked Jameson on his side. He curled into a ball, anticipating further rough use.

"This isn't personal, Herbert," Gilbert said.

"I don't know where it came from!" Jameson cried as two soldiers hauled him to his feet.

"I don't think they believe you," Gilbert said. "I certainly don't."

Once the castle had a pit into which evildoers had been cast, but that pit had been filled in long ago, for it took up valuable storage space in one of the towers. But the castle still needed a place to keep prisoners, so a spot had been cleared in one of the buildings lining the east wall of the outer bailey, and shackles put into the walls on the ground floor. At the moment, the cell held two murderers, four robbers, and seven rapists awaiting the return of the crown justice for this area, Ademar de Valence, who had found urgent business in London at the outbreak of hostilities last November. This rash of crime had used up the available shackles, so the manacles applied to Herbert Jameson had been entwined with those of one of the murderers. Neither found the arrangement comfortable.

Jameson continued to protest his innocence while Gilbert and Turling waited for one of the soldiers to return with the thumbscrew, which was kept in the pantry behind old loaves of bread designated as alms for the poor. Gilbert would have preferred to rely on relentless questioning to break Jameson down, but once Turling got involved, the prospect of torture had become inevitable.

However, at the appearance of the thumbscrew, Jameson threw himself prostrate on the floor, as much as his manacled wrists and the murderer's chain would allow, and cried for mercy.

"You can have mercy if you tell me where you got the sword," Turling said.

Jameson was bawling so that when he spoke, he could not be understood.

Turling set the thumbscrew by one of Jameson's hands. He grasped a wrist, and said, "You'll have to do better than that."

Gilbert knelt as well and wiped Jameson's face and the drool that hung from his lips. "Come now, Herbert. Calm yourself. Take a deep breath. That's better. Now, about the sword . . ."

"I-i-it w-w-was S-S-Simon," Jameson stammered. "He gave it to me."

Gilbert and Turling exchanged glances. "You were right," Turling said.

"Where did he get it?" Gilbert asked.

"He found it in the yard."

"That's hard to believe."

"It's true! I swear! He had nothing to do with Ormyn's death!"

"Whether that's true or not remains to be seen," Gilbert said.

"You'll let me go now?" Jameson blubbered.

"I think not," Turling said. "Dealing in stolen property is a serious crime."

"I'm entitled to bail!" Jameson cried.

"In due time, perhaps," Turling replied. "Come along, Gilbert. Let's finish this unpleasant business."

Before fetching Herbert Jameson, Gilbert and Turling had taken the precaution of arresting his brother Simon for questioning. Simon had been placed in the town gaol so that the brothers would not have the chance to see each other and, perhaps, fix their stories. The gaol consisted of a small room at the back of the guildhall. There was no telling its original purpose now, but its employment as a gaol seemed an afterthought, as it was near the back door and could easily be reached from the outside by anyone skilled at latch jimmying. Moreover, the town did not splurge on a full time guard, that cost being viewed as excessive and unnecessary. So the door was merely locked, with the key in the possession of the town clerk, Edmund Tarbent.

"We'll have to move him," Turling said, as he and Gilbert passed through the hall to the corridor leading to the gaol. "It's not safe to keep a murderer here."

"If he's the one," Gilbert said.

"He has to be the one. It's obvious, isn't it?"

"It looks more and more likely. But what seems likely sometimes turns out not to be true."

"Well," Turling grunted as they turned the corner. "what are you doing here? Getting your stories straight? There! You see?" He gestured down the passageway, where Bridget Yarker had stepped back from the gaol's door. Behind her the back door to the hall stood open where she had neglected to close it.

"What are you doing here, Mistress Yarker?" Gilbert asked as they reached Bridget.

"I heard that Simon had been arrested. Why?" Bridget's manner was bold, but it seemed to contain more bluster than actual courage.

"We suspect him in the death of your late husband."

Turling grunted. "Wistwode may suspect your husband, but I know you had a hand in this deviltry. You put him up to it — confess!"

"I did no such thing!" Bridget cried.

"You told me often enough how tired you were of Ormyn," Turling said.

"She did?" Gilbert asked, feeling the ground shifting.

Turling sneered. "When I came here, she threw herself at my feet. I admit I had a go at her, but it was only for a few weeks. She's a boring girl, really. A farmer's daughter who thinks too much of herself. But it was long enough to hear the catalogue of complaints she had about Ormyn."

"I see," Gilbert said. "Why didn't you say you suspected she had a hand in Ormyn's death? As I recall, you said he had no enemies."

Turling's mouth curled. "I did not suspect that her unhappiness would take such a turn — until she moved in with Simon while Ormyn was still warm — and Ormyn's sword turns up in Jameson's possession."

"I must admit, that is damning evidence. But there might be a harmless explanation. We must inquire, hear their side of things. Perhaps this evidence can be explained."

"I'll have a confession out of Jameson before the day's over. That will be evidence enough."

"It is amazing to me that you have managed to keep this affair a secret until now," Gilbert said to Bridget. "Castles are such small places and secrets like this are hard to conceal. What were you doing, using the Pigeon as a trysting place? You may as well tell us. We'll find out eventually."

Bridge was quiet for a moment. "On Sundays. We all went for bowls on Sundays. Herb gave Simon and me a room for an hour while Ormyn threw his pay away."

"Ormyn never suspected a thing, then," Gilbert said. "The poor fellow."

"Poor my ass," Bridget spat. "He was a monster."

Gilbert blinked in surprise. "A monster? That is a heavy charge."

"He beat me and the children over the smallest thing. A cup out of place on the table could set him off. Always in debt because of that place, always quick with his fists whenever I objected."

There was a ring of falsehood and exaggeration in the accusation about the beatings, and Gilbert wasn't sure whether to believe this, after what he had learned about Bridget from Sally. But he tried to keep an open mind.

"She has just condemned herself, and Simon," Turling declared. "They both had reason to be rid of Ormyn. They must have conspired together."

"I doubt that little Bridget here could heave her husband off the wall by herself," Gilbert agreed.

"I didn't! I swear!" Bridget cried, and through the door came Simon's voice, for he had heard every word: "She's innocent! We're both innocent! I took the sword, I admit it! But I didn't kill him! We didn't!"

"Unlock the door," Turling commanded the soldier with the key. "Let's hear this face to face."

The soldier fumbled with the lock and stood back as the door opened. Simon filled the doorway. Bridget slapped him hard. "You took his sword, and you didn't tell me!"

Simon put his hand to his face. "I saw his body from the wall the morning after. If anyone knew I had the sword, I knew I'd be accused."

"So how did you come into possession of it?" Gilbert asked.

"I found it," Simon said.

"That is the most implausible thing I have ever heard," Gilbert said.

"I did. In the yard."

"By yard, what do you mean? The inner bailey or the outer?"

"The inner of course. We both had duty that night. On the same watch."

"Where in the inner yard?"

"By the chapel."

Gilbert thought for a moment. "Sir Ralph, I would like to have him show us exactly where he contends he found the sword."

"What for?"

"I think this detail may be important somehow. I would like to see the place with my own eyes rather have to rely on Jameson's description."

"You mean, let him out?" Turling asked. "He could escape."

"Not surrounded by so many men. Shackle his feet. That will slow him down enough even for a baby to catch him."

Shackles could not be found in the guildhall, but a length of rope was used to tie Simon's feet together as a horse was hobbled. Soldiers held Simon's arms, and the party left the hall, with soldiers on either side of Bridget as well.

There weren't many people on High Street, but Gilbert did not spot a single one who failed to gawk at the spectacle of a hobbled Simon being led toward the castle.

The castle wards at the gate gawked as well, seeing one of their number treated in this way. One asked Turling as they passed, "Sir, what's going on?"

But Turling's grim expression did not alter, nor did he respond. If Turling would not answer, none of the others felt daring enough to do so either, apart from a whispered, "We'll tell you later."

Turling halted at the doorway to the chapel within the inner bailey. "Ask your questions," he said to Gilbert.

"All right, Simon," Gilbert said. "Where did you find the sword?"

"There." Simon pointed to a spot along the north wall of the chapel.

"Perhaps you should walk over and show me the exact spot."

Simon hobbled along the wall and halted beneath one of the windows. "It was here."

Gilbert glanced up, counting the number of windows. The place Simon indicated was the one Stephen said belonged to the chamber where the relic had been kept. "And how did you happen to find it here? You said you were on watch that night."

"I was on the wall, there." Simon gestured toward the west wall on the other side of the bailey. "A messenger arrived. There was quite a flurry of attention at it, people coming out with torches and such, grooms attending to his horse. I saw it lying there on the ground in the light of the torches."

"Did you know it for what it was?"

"That it belonged to Ormyn? Not until I fetched it."

"And you didn't wonder what it was doing there?"

"Oh, I wondered all right."

"But you didn't seek him out to return it."

There was a pause. "No. I didn't."

"You were determined to keep it."

Simon nodded, glancing apprehensively at Bridget.

"You fancied it," Gilbert said.

Simon nodded again.

"Like you fancied his wife," Turling growled. "You bastard. I don't believe this fairy tale. The long and the short of it is, you killed him for the sword and for his wife."

"I swear, I didn't kill him!"

"So I take it that you hid the sword until you could get it safely out of the castle and into your brother's hands," Gilbert said.

Simon nodded a third time. "I thought no one would find it there." He then added, "I heard voices that night."

"Voices?" Gilbert echoed.

"Coming from over there." Simon waved a hand at the wall walk above and behind the hall's roof. "It sounded like

Ormyn, and another. They didn't speak long. It could have been the wind. At least, I thought so at the time. When I went up there, I saw no one."

"This is getting us nowhere," Turling said. "I'll have the truth out of you in short order. Take him to the gaol. We'll question him there."

The soldiers marched Simon toward the gate to the outer bailey, with Turling following, hands behind his back. Gilbert and Bridget remained by the chapel.

"Aren't you coming?" Turling called.

"No," Gilbert said. "I think I've heard enough."

"They're going to hurt him, aren't they?" Bridget asked as she too was led away.

"I imagine they are."

"If you believe him then you'd stop it."

"Do you believe him?"

"Yes, despite what he did, I do."

"I think I believe him as well, oddly enough, even though I hardly see a reason to do so. But I'm just a clerk. I have no power over Turling and his sort." Gilbert turned away, feeling sorry for Simon and no closer to the solution of Ormyn's death than he had been when he started.

The screams began as Gilbert reached the main gate. He paused and turned back toward the sounds, his stomach writhing with dismay, and was about to hurry out of earshot when he saw Herbert Jameson approaching, head down, hands over his ears. Space in the castle gaol was too precious for keeping the likes of him, and he had been released for now.

"That bastard!" Jameson spat as he reached Gilbert.

"That is one word one might use to describe him," Gilbert said as he fell alongside as best he could, as eager as Jameson to get as far away from the screaming as he could.

Jameson stopped just beyond the gate and turned on Gilbert. "I warned Simon not to have anything to do with her!"

"With Bridget?"

"She worked for a time at the Pigeon after those who run the Crow threw her out. She was trouble, always complaining about this or that. Nothing was ever good enough where she was concerned. It was enough to make your head burst, sometimes. I was glad when Ormyn took her away. I think I'd have killed her if I had to listen to her whining and carrying on one minute longer. Then Ormyn took to bringing her along when he played bowls. To keep an eye on her, I suppose. He was a wee bit jealous. I guess he had cause, because it weren't long before she winked at Simon and he was lost from that moment. I warned him to have nothing to do with her. But he didn't listen, the weak-kneed fool. I like to think our mother didn't raise no fools, but he turned into one where Bridget was concerned, damn him. There's nothing we can do for Simon now, is there?"

"I wish there were."

"What the hell good are you, then?" Jameson spat and left Gilbert standing in High Street.

"Not good for much, I suppose," Gilbert said to himself. "Not good for much at all."

Chapter 19

"Do you really think Bridget might be involved?" Gilbert asked Stephen for at least the third time. The pair huddled by the fireplace while night fell and the temperature dropped on the evening of Stephen's return from Montgomery.

"I don't know," Stephen said. He hugged his cloak about his shoulders, and stared into the flames, trying to put his thoughts in order about what he must do now that it was clear he was not going to find the relic. Selling a horse was the first thing to do. He shrank from such a decision, but it was the only way to get enough money to tide him over until he found another position. "It's not my affair now."

"It's a pity you feel that way. Simon's life, and Bridget's as well, depend on what we do. You're going to leave them to their fates? Turling's convinced that Bridget is guilty, even if Simon hasn't implicated her so far. What if they are innocent after all?"

"What else am I going to do? Parfet's dead. The trail is cold. FitzAllen will be back in a month or six weeks. The campaign isn't going to last much longer than that. I'll be arrested on one pretext or another. My life's worth about as much as Jameson's if that happens."

"When will you go, then?"

"I'll have to raise some money first. Sir Geoff's late on our salaries again."

"You'll follow Harry's advice?"

"When market day comes round again. I should have sold a horse when the army was here. I'd probably have got a better price for her. Can't be helped now. The sooner I'm out of here, the better."

"Edith will miss you."

"No, she won't. She'll be glad to have her chamber back. What favor did my cousin do for you that it's cost you so much to make amends?"

"I'd rather not go into that. It was an unsavory business."

"Knowing you, it must have been bad indeed."

"Don't make light of my troubles. I don't make light of yours."

"Your pardon."

"Granted." After a pause, Gilbert added, "Perhaps if we sleep on it, the solution will come. You've a few days left to give it one last try."

"All right, I shall sleep on it." Stephen sat back, feeling oddly better. Although the trails seemed to have gone cold and the thrill of the hunt had diminished, a glimmer of the thrill still smoldered. It was harder to let go of than he had anticipated.

The solutions to the mysteries did not seem any clearer as Stephen awoke the next morning. When he turned his thoughts to the matter as he washed in his basin, his mind filled with uncertainty. It was not a satisfactory way to start the day.

He pulled on a shirt before throwing open the shutters to dump out the wash water. As he upended the basin, he noticed Harry sitting by the stable door in the same place he usually occupied to take the rising sun on Sundays. But this was a Tuesday.

"What are you still doing here?" Stephen called down.

Harry glanced up with a sour expression and did not respond. Without his beard it was much easier to read his moods, although sourness seemed to predominate when he wasn't trying to look pathetic. Yet there was something more than the usual indisposition in it.

Stephen finished dressing and descended to the hall, where he appropriated a trencher of bread and cheese which he carried out to the yard. He sat next to Harry. "Had your breakfast yet?"

Harry's eyes flicked up then fell away. "Jennie was out with it earlier."

Stephen expected Harry to snatch a piece of bread or cheese, but his hands did not move from his lap. Stephen bit into a hunk of cheese, which proved to be older and harder than anticipated. "You want to talk about it?"

"Talk about what?"

"Whatever's bothering you. You ill or something?"

"No. I'm fine. Everything's fine. The world's fine, which means it's as fucked up as usual."

"Hmm. You and Jennie have a fight?"

"No, we're a pair of love birds."

"Well, I am surprised that neither Edith nor Gilbert have noticed that."

"Gilbert's too thick. I worry more about Edith. . . . All hell's going to break loose today."

"You mean your infatuation is now public knowledge? And that she's going to hear of it?"

"Not that. We both been attainted, Jennie and me."

Stephen was surprised to hear this. Attainment was the formal bringing of a charge of wrongdoing. He could not imagine what the both of them had done. "Well, I know you are the criminal sort, but Jennie! What have to done to lead her to crime?"

"We've been selling these little carvings I've been making, or rather I make them and she sells them to travelers at the inn and a few townsfolk here and there. We split the profits."

Stephen saw the nature of the offense clearly now. "So a bailiff caught you, eh?"

Harry nodded. "No license for commerce. You've got to have a license to take a shit in this town."

"That doesn't explain why you're sitting here when you should be at Broad Gate."

"The bailiff told me my beggar's permit was suspended. For doing business in violation. Said he'd have me arrested if he caught me there."

"That is unfortunate." It was, in fact, more than unfortunate. It was a disaster from Harry's point of view. He had no means now of supporting himself.

"Unfortunate." Harry dragged the word out to three times its normal length. "That's a clever way of putting it."

"So when did this happen?"

"Late yesterday. Word's not got around to here yet. But it won't be long. Do you think she'll throw me out?"

"That is a possibility. I believe she regards you as a bad influence on young Jennie."

"She's always wanted a reason to be rid of me."

"You are taking up valuable space, after all."

"You are not cheering me up."

"I was not put here on earth to cheer people up. That's Gilbert's job. Do you have any of your savings left?"

"Course I do. Why?"

"It seems to me that the prudent course is to throw yourself on the town clerk's mercy and pay your fine and Jennie's before Edith finds out about this."

Harry considered this plan for a moment. "All right. But that bastard Tarbent will want a bribe." Edmund Tarbent, the town clerk, was as grasping a man as ever held any position of authority.

"Of course he will. But that's how justice is obtained."

"I can't just go clumping around Ludlow with all that money. I'll need a bodyguard."

"As I am not otherwise occupied this morning, I suppose I could accompany you. The fresh air will do me good."

"Fresh air? In Ludlow?"

"Fresher than here, certainly. That privy does stink a bit, doesn't it?"

"It should, considering what's in it."

It would have taken a long time for Harry to climb Broad Street to High, and then along its length to the guild hall upon his board, so Stephen summoned one of the servants, the boy Mark, to haul Harry in the handcart. Mark disliked this chore because he loathed Harry, and Harry didn't like it because it cost him a farthing that he could ill afford.

"You're pretty free with my money," Harry complained as Stephen heaved him onto the bed of the cart.

"Quit your complaining. I am about to resolve all your troubles."

"Not all of them," Harry said, settling onto the cart.

"You'll have to take care of your love life by yourself."

"What are you talking about?" Mark asked.

"None of your business," Harry snapped.

"If he's going to be rude to me again, I'll have none of this," Mark said, "no matter what you're paying."

"It is a private matter," Stephen said. "Harry's entitled to his secrets like anyone else. Now, let's get going."

Mark took up the handles and jerked with such force that Harry nearly toppled backward out of the cart.

"Easy there!" Harry cried.

"Ha!" Mark declared, making for the gate almost at a trot, the cart jolting to and fro over the uneven ground. "Give me any sass now, and you'll know what for!"

"Stephen! Do something about this wretched boy!"

"Mark," Stephen admonished, "behave."

"Of course, sir," Mark said with a wicked backward grin. "I'm behaving as well as he's entitled."

"If I die, it's your fault." Harry glared at Stephen. "Oh! You think this is funny, do you?"

"Me? No. Of course not."

Despite the precariousness of the conveyance, Harry reached the guild hall on High Street in one piece without falling off the cart, although the turn at the corner with Broad Street was a near thing as Mark charged it with extra vigor. Perhaps the fact that there were people at Spicers' wines shop who witnessed this had something to do with it, since they found the spectacle of Harry clinging to the bouncing cart to be very amusing and called insults through the windows.

When they reached the guild hall, Mark dropped the cart handles, which caused the cart to pitch forward and would have tossed Harry to the ground if Stephen hadn't caught his shoulder. Four of the town bailiffs were lounging on a bench beneath the overhang formed by the the hall's first floor, which jutted out from the rest of the building. They took in Mark's performance with appreciation. One of them said, "What you doing here, Harry? Seeing the sights? You're awful far from your usual haunts."

"No," Harry said through gritted teeth as he let himself down from the cart, "I've come for justice after the mean-spirited thing you've done."

"What, me?" the bailiff said. "I was just enforcing the law. You was flouting it. God knows what else you're up to when our backs are turned. We've heard you've even been seen speaking with Will Thumper. Bad company, that one."

"Is Tarbent about?" Stephen butted in before this exchange could go somewhere that it should not.

A bailiff waved at the chamber overhead. "He's at his books, sir, as usual."

"More likely at his wine, as usual," another bailiff said.

"Hush!" the third bailiff said. "He might hear."

"Oh, yes," the one who had spoken about wine replied, a finger on his lips. "I forgot."

"Thanks," Stephen said, taking the bag of Harry's savings from the cart. "Come along, Harry."

He entered the hall and crossed to the stairs at the back which climbed to the first floor. He was several steps up before he realized that Harry was not following. Harry sat at the bottom, contemplating the stairs with some dismay.

"They are rather steep, aren't they?" Stephen commented, descending to the ground. "I'd forgotten about them."

"You can't ask him to come down, can you?" Harry asked.

"It will put him in a foul mood."

"He's always in a foul mood."

"Well, a mood fouler than usual."

"You could give me some assistance," Harry said. "Like you did on the way back from the Kettle, on the day it rained."

There was, fortunately, no one about, so Stephen squatted down to enable Harry to grasp his shoulders. Then he stood up with Harry on his back and climbed the stairs.

The levying of fines was not the town clerk's role, strictly speaking. His formal job was to record the attainders so that the appropriate manor court — the town being jointly owned by the Genevilles and the Verduns — could impose any fine when it met once a month. But in practice, the clerk was allowed to collect fines for minor offenses and remove the attainder as long as enough of a fine found its way back to the manor, in this instance the Genevilles since the offenses had occurred in their section of Ludlow, with the clerk pocketing a small amount for his expenses.

Thus it was that Stephen and Harry emerged onto High Street with Harry's savings considerably depleted. At least Harry's beggar's license was restored, although he had to endure a lecture from Tarbent about how one could not simultaneously be a businessman and a beggar on Tarbent's watch; he had to choose one or the other. Surprisingly, Harry had endured this lecture without comment.

Harry was pulling himself onto the bed of the cart, which Mark steadied so that it would not tip over, although the bailiffs called encouragement for him to let go at the most precarious instant, when two of the castle guards hurrying along High Street caught sight of Stephen and shouted his name.

The guards jogged up and paused, out of breath from their haste, to the seated bailiff's amazement. "Sir Stephen!" one of them burst out. "You must come. We've been looking all over for you."

Stephen's heart sank. This sort of anxious summons could mean only one thing. "Who's died now?"

"It's Simon — Simon Jameson!" the guard cried.

"He's hanged himself!" cried the other.

"Hanged himself?" Stephen asked. "You're quite sure?" To be truthful, he would not have been surprised to hear of Jameson's death, but he supposed it would come another way: such as from infection setting in after Turling's rough treatment. But hanging? That was a rare thing indeed. He'd only once before seen an instance where a person hanged herself, and the girl had been driven to it by despair at a lover's betrayal and death.

"We saw him ourselves."

"Happened last night, had to've been."

"All right, then, let's go see him," Stephen said with resignation. The little sense of satisfaction he had experienced at solving Harry's and Jennie's problem had been whisked away, even though he wanted to hang onto it for a few moments longer.

When Stephen passed through the castle gate, someone in the crowd around the entrance to the gaol spotted him, and everyone turned in his direction. The jurymen and Gilbert were already there, and it was apparent that they had been waiting for him.

"Where have you been?" Gilbert asked. "I've had people looking all over for you."

"Harry and I had some business to take care of," Stephen said, aware that Mark, curious as anyone about this event, had followed with Harry and the cart.

Gilbert glanced at Harry. "What sort of business?"

"It's nothing. A problem with his license. It's taken care of now." Before Gilbert could inquire further, in case he had heard about Jennie, Stephen went on, "What happened. Do we know?"

"It seems pretty straightforward. See for yourself."

Stephen went to the doorway. He hesitated before going in because the stink of shit and piss was so strong that he almost gagged. He swallowed and entered. There were eight men chained to rings imbedded in the walls, some more tattered looking than others. Jameson's body was to the right. He had looped a belt through the ring securing his neck chain and hung himself from that, even though the ring was no more than four feet or so from the ground. He looked, in fact, as though he had sat down on a chair, which someone had removed. Stephen felt Jameson's jaw. It was still rigid.

"He died sometime in the middle of the night, a couple of hours before dawn, maybe," Stephen said.

Gilbert nodded his agreement.

"Did any of you see or hear anything?" Stephen asked the prisoners.

"We didn't see nor hear nothing," one of them said.

Stephen wasn't sure he believed this, but a round of bobbing heads suggested it might take some work to get them to say anything different. "Nobody came in?"

"That door makes a racket," another prisoner said. "No way you can sleep through that. 'Sides, nobody comes in here after supper. Ever."

"So he just hung himself last night and none of you noticed?"

"Nope," several said at once. "Didn't see or hear nothing. We was fast asleep."

"Have him cut down and laid in the yard," Stephen ordered Gilbert.

Gilbert cut off Jameson's clothes down to his braises, and he and Stephen went over every visible inch of the dead man's skin.

After they finished, Gilbert sighed, "No bruises other than the mark left by the belt."

"Unlikely there was a struggle, then," Stephen said. "Although he couldn't have put up much resistant with his hand like that." Four of the fingers on Jameson's right hand were crushed, the tips bloody and swollen to the size of small balls, the nails gone from two of them.

Gilbert turned the dead man's head. He pointed to the base of the skull. "See how the mark rises up from beneath the chin to the rear of the head? That's consistent with a hanging rather than strangulation. Why would he have taken such a step?" Suicide, while not unheard of, was a rare and terrible thing.

"To save himself from more torture," Stephen said. "Turling wasn't done with him, was he?"

"No. He hadn't got out of Simon all that he wanted."

"Perhaps it wasn't the prospect of pain. Perhaps he feared that he would give up Bridget."

Gilbert looked surprised at this suggestion, for it had not occurred to him. "That could be it," he mused. "In fact, I think you're right. He loved her to the end. A pity that she probably does not return the feeling."

Stephen stood up and looked at the jurymen, who had crowded around to watch the examination. "You've seen the body. I assume you've already spoken to the prisoners?"

"And to the watch," said Thomas Tanner, one of the jury.

"All right, then, what's your judgment?"

Chapter 20

Harry was still by the doorway to the stable when Stephen brought the stallion out first thing in the morning and tied its halter rope to one of the rings by the door. There would be practice today at the castle, as there was every weekday, and since it was a Thursday they would be working on mounted skills. For the first time since he had left Spain, he would try jousting at the quintain and perhaps some mock combat with staves on horseback. He was looking forward to that.

"What are you still doing here?" Stephen asked as he lifted a fore hoof to pick out the dirt.

"Waiting for my breakfast," Harry said. "The girl is late. Second day in a row." He glanced sourly at the house and bent over another carving. It had proved impossible to keep secret the fact of Jennie's attainder and the cause of it, and Edith had decreed that Jennie was to have nothing to do with Harry in future. Even the fact that he had spent most of his savings to pay her fine did not blunt Edith's determination. Consequently, Jennie and Harry had not got within fifty feet of one another since the row. "Gilbert says you're leaving."

Stephen put down the hoof and started on another. "In a couple of weeks, I think. When things have quieted down and I can fetch Christopher."

"That stirrup work all right for you, then?"

"Like old times."

"Nothing holding you back now, I suppose. Prance around a bit on that horse and kiss the right asses, and you'll get that earldom yet."

"No, there isn't, although I doubt there's an earldom in my future. I'll settle for a nice, comfortable manor." Nothing physical kept him here now, that much was true. However, there was still this nagging feeling of having left things undone, of the hunt uncompleted, of crucial pieces distantly perceived but not understood, and of things about to be left behind that, to his surprise, he did not want to part with. It left Stephen dissatisfied and out of sorts.

"Lucky for you," Harry said.

"I suppose it is." Stephen resisted the impulse to tell Harry that things could look up for him in future as well. But Harry would not believe him, and he would be right to do so. Nothing could change things for Harry. He had sunk as low as anyone could possibly sink and there would be no rising up for him, ever.

The door to the house opened and one of the serving girls came across the yard with a trencher. She put it on the bench beside him and lingered a moment over the carving in Harry's hand. "That's very good," she said. "Is it the saint?"

"No," Harry said.

"It looks familiar."

"It's nobody you know."

Since Harry didn't seem sociable enough to go on, the girl retreated to the house.

"Still at it, eh?" Stephen asked as he finished with the hooves and began currying and brushing the horse.

"It occupies the mind. Say, did you know that the wake's today?"

"Wake? What wake?" Although as soon as Stephen spoke he knew.

"For Simon Jameson. His brother's holding a wake this morning at the Pigeon. I hear there'll be free food and drink."

"You thinking about going?"

"Nah. No way to get there from Broad Gate. Herb's going to plant Simon by the Corve, they say. Nice place to be buried, don't you think? Good view, quiet and near the bowls."

"Why would being near the bowls matter?" Normally, people wanted to bury their loved ones in consecrated ground, but Simon being a suicide made that impossible.

"Simon loved his bowls. Him and Ormyn used to play at every opportunity."

Something tickled at the edge of Stephen's mind, like a name on the tip of his tongue. "Are you sure Simon liked bowls? I thought he went only so he could have a go at Bridget."

Harry smiled, examining the carving. "That was just a useful byproduct of his obsession. Herb didn't offer bowls at all until Simon talked him into it." He held out the carving to Stephen. "Would you mind giving this to Jennie when you see her?"

Stephen took the carving. It was not of the girl in the ice, as Harry had said. It was of Jennie herself. "I'll be glad to, Harry."

No one had mentioned Simon's wake when Stephen was at the castle on Wednesday, and no one mentioned it this morning. But at the close of practice, half the complement shed their arms, and when they were in High Street only then did someone bring up the subject as they were about to part ways with Stephen.

"You're going?" Stephen asked, surprised to learn the group's destination.

"Not all of us believe he killed Ormyn," one of the guards said.

"That bastard, Turling," another of them muttered.

"You coming or not?" the first guard asked.

"I believe I will," Stephen said.

"Do you think he killed Ormyn, sir?" the guard asked. "Owing to the fact that I know you've made inquiries."

"No, I don't think he did."

"But who was it, then?"

"I wish I knew," Stephen said, his disquiet and discontent stirring.

Stephen and Gilbert heard the tumult of the crowd even before they reached the corner at Saint Leonard's chapel and turned onto Linney Lane.

The crowd was much larger than Stephen had expected, and far from somber. It filled the yard so that it seemed anyone anxious to bowl lacked the cleared space for a cast, and spilled into the lane; here and there the pressure of the crowd had collapse the wicker fence lining the road and facilitated the crowd's expansion. Its mood was boisterous, as if this was a feast day instead of an occasion for mourning.

"Not a bad send off," Stephen observed.

"They're local boys. Both grew up here about Linney crossing," Gilbert said as he stopped short. "I don't think this is a good idea."

"Why not?" Stephen asked.

"The role I played in Simon's death. Jameson may hold an extra measure of resentment. So may his friends. I see quite a few of them here, the whole neighborhood, in fact."

"You fear a beating?"

"Or worse."

"They'll have to answer to me."

"I appreciate your protection — I suppose. Although last time there was trouble, it didn't save me from a near roasting," Gilbert said, recalling his escape from Earl Percival FitzAllen's gaol last autumn, which had been set afire by Welsh attackers while he and Stephen were still inside.

"Last time no part of you was even singed. All you got was a minor fright, and I've seen you have those in the yard over stray cats. Come along. I need your eyes and ears, if not that head of yours. There's something I've missed. I don't know what it is, but if I can't think of it, perhaps you can."

"It's hard to give anything deep thought when you're in grave danger," Gilbert muttered, but he did not resist Stephen tug on the sleeve.

Once through the gate and among the crowd, Gilbert relaxed a bit. Perhaps it was the fact he was shorter than most men and therefore didn't stand out, or that he had put up his hood which made his face hard to see unless he was standing in front of anyone. Although the weather was mild and it was a bit unusual to put up a hood, no one paid him any attention, and they were able to acquire cups of ale without being challenged. A pig had been roasted and there was still some of it left, so they got some chunks of pork, which they supplemented with boiled eggs from a bucket near the head, some cheese, and bread.

"The pork could use some salt," Gilbert muttered as he chewed.

"It's free," Stephen said. "Don't complain."

"If it was my pig, I'd have allowed for salt."

"If Edith would let you. Come on, let's watch the bowls." There was a game going on at the farthest pitch.

"I didn't think you were a fan of bowls."

"I'm not. Never was any good at the game. My brother, he was the bowler. Always took the prize at the Ludlow fair, or almost always, anyway, before he got respectable and his wife made him give it up."

They had not been long at the game when Herbert Jameson mounted a table and called for quiet. He cleared his throat and put his hands on his hips, lips compressed as though he had to nerve himself up to speak to the crowd. "I know that you'd much rather eat and drink — and watch the bowls if you're not playing — but we all know we're here for more than just the fun. We're here to remember my brother, Simon, and to give him the kind of send off that he would have appreciated. Now I know he wouldn't have appreciated speeches any more than you do, but I must say a few words. I won't be long, so you can stand still and be quiet until I'm done.

"This has been a bad year for bowls in Ludlow. We've lost some of our best bowlers — not only Simon, but Ormyn Yarker and Wace Bursecot — all men cruelly cut down when their best games lay ahead of them. The pitch will never be the same without them, nor the wagering as fierce and hot. How many among you have lost money to those fellows, eh?"

A shout went up, and as it died someone called, "And some of us are still owed money!"

"And if it's Simon's debt, I'll make it good!" Herbert Jameson called. He lifted his cup. "So! To Simon, that poor bastard, and also to Ormyn, and even to Wace, I say, may their stones roll straight and true up above at that great pitch in Heaven!"

"Here! Here!" the crowd shouted in answer, cups raised and then emptied.

"All right, then!" Jameson said. "We've still a little pig left, and there are some honey cakes straight from the oven down the street that haven't had a chance to cool yet! Finish up! There's a fresh grave that needs filling and we can't get on with that until the food's gone." He hopped from the table.

Gilbert turned toward Stephen whose face was screwed up. Gilbert pounded him on the back, thinking he had a piece of pig caught in his throat, when in fact it was a thought that had almost come clear as Jameson had delivered his speech.

"Are you all right, lad?" Gilbert asked anxiously. "Can you speak?"

"Wagers," Stephen said.

"What?"

"Wagers — wagers and bowls."

"All right," Gilbert ventured. "They go together, usually."

"Parfet was a bowler. Remember, we saw him here."

"But you said you didn't think he had anything to do with anything. If he had stolen the relic, he wouldn't have needed to go on that ill-fated raid."

"No, but Melmerby may have done."

"Melmerby? Who's that?"

"I forgot. You wouldn't know. He was Parfet's valet or chamberlain, or something. I was never quite clear on what. But he was always at Parfet's side, except at the end."

Gilbert drew a breath. "So Melmerby would have been there, in Wattepas' shop, and seen the emeralds."

"Yes, he had to have been."

"But what does this have to do with wagers and bowls?"

"Melmerby was a great bowler. He won almost three shillings from me, although I never paid it."

"Stephen!"

"He died. Mysteriously. I told you."

"I still do not get the connection."

"Melmerby had to have played here. Which means he probably played with Ormyn and Wace —"

"— and probably won."

"Yes."

"And so . . .?"

"Wace knew where the monks had put the relic for safekeeping. He could have been induced to reveal the hiding place as payment for his debt."

"And Ormyn? How does he come into this?"

"He was a climber, remember? It would take a good climber to get in and out of that window. And Simon said he found Ormyn's sword by the chapel's north wall. He must have given it to Melmerby to hold so as not to be encumbered."

"Then that messenger came in and caused a commotion, with people rushing about bearing torches which will have lit up the entire bailey."

"Right. Melmerby dropped the sword at the surprise and they fled up the stairs to the east wall, leaving it there on the ground beneath the very window to the relic's hiding place."

"Does that mean Melmerby killed Ormyn?"

"He is the only possible suspect. Imagine it — they get to the wall walk behind the hall where they can't be seen and Ormyn finds that Melmerby has left his sword behind. Ormyn will naturally believe that will incriminate him. They argue. Perhaps Ormyn wants to go back and retrieve it. Melmerby hits Ormyn as much to shut him up as anything. Remember, Ormyn had been struck on the jaw. He had the same sort of injury a man gets from a blow from a fist. The blow leaves Ormyn dazed. Melmerby impulsively throws him over the wall — thus ridding himself of the only witness to his crime and avoiding the need to share any of its proceeds."

Gilbert was quiet, contemplating what Stephen had proposed. "I suppose that might mean Melmerby is also responsible for Wace's death, although I don't see how that could have happened."

"You said Wace left the Pigeon suddenly after seeing something on the road."

"Yes, I recall saying that."

"Parfet's company left town that morning at about that time. Wace could have seen them. He could have been promised money from the sale of the relic in addition to cancelling of his debt. The sight of Melmerby leaving might have alarmed him into thinking he had been cheated. Melmerby was a reckless man. I learned that much about him."

"It's all just speculation, though, isn't it? We have no proof, and shall never see any at this point, I expect. Amusing to think about, but it gets us no nearer to the solution of any of these terrible events."

"There is one more thing."

"What?"

"Will Thumper said that the men who came to the tunnel that night had a shovel."

"Ah, a shovel. You never mentioned that."

"I had forgotten. The thought of graves and digging brought it to mind. Melmerby would have known that he couldn't sell the relic in Ludlow. He also would have known that the army would leave soon, and he couldn't afford to carry such a thing into Wales."

"He didn't go to Wales. He went to Montgomery."

"He wouldn't have known that's where he would end up. Anyway, reckless as he was, I doubt he would have chanced taking it to Montgomery, either."

"So he hid it somewhere. That's helpful. We shall now have to scour the woods looking for holes in the ground, as if someone of his sort would leave obvious holes."

"Maybe we don't have that far to look."

"I have never taken you as an optimist."

"Finding the dark lining to every silver cloud is Harry's forte. No, Thumper also said that his visitors went away toward the Dinham Bridge."

"Ah, that narrows things down to only a few hundred acres or so."

"How would you hide something in the night, expecting to come back for it before long? You wouldn't just walk into the woods and dig a hole any old place. You'd want to put it near a landmark that would be easily remembered."

"Whitcliff is not far away from the Dinham Bridge and it's very hard to miss."

"You'd stumble up there in the dark? Besides, it's too big. You'd want something like a peculiar rock or tree . . . or the bridge itself."

"The bridge itself?"

"The bridge is hard to miss in the dark. And you said Wace was found under the Corve Bridge. People don't ordinarily go poking around under bridges."

"Well, I have enjoyed your speculations, but there is a flaw."

"Flaw? What flaw?"

"It is easily checked. I hate to leave this wonderful wake, with all this free food and drink, but your speculation cries out for refutation." Gilbert stood up. "What are you waiting for?"

As they wended their way toward the gate, Stephen said, "You know, there is one thing about you that has always wounded me."

"What is that?"

"You question everything I say."

"You are so often wrong, after all. And I wouldn't call it questioning; it is a fine and gentle guiding hand leading you away from error."

"If I prove to be correct, you shall not do so for a full month. Agreed?"

"And if I win, you shall clean the privy."

"You are a cruel little man."

"I am a man soon to have a clean privy at no cost to me."

Chapter 21

There had been talk among the town elders of building a stone bridge across the Teme at Dinham to replace the wooden one, which was in need of repair, with rotting planks along its length posing a threat to commerce, not to mention life and limb. But so far no one had been able to mount enough enthusiasm for the expense, so the bridge, gray and rickety, still spanned the river just below the Dinham mill at the same spot where it had stood for at least a century and maybe more. Perhaps no stick of wood in its construction had survived that long, as most had been replaced piecemeal as they had worn out, but it looked like nothing had changed since it had first been put up.

The bridge provided a tranquil sight as Stephen and Gilbert came around the northwest corner of the castle on the cart track connecting Linney with the mill, and they could see it through the green haze of the budding trees. The wheel creaked with the rapid flow of the high water brought on by the spring melt, and there were several carts in the mill yard as people had brought their corn for grinding to take advantage of the flow — in summer and autumn when water was low and you could see the rocks on the bottom of the river, there often wasn't enough current to turn the mill even with much of the river diverted by weirs.

The only odd thing about the view was a curl of smoke coming from below the foot of the bridge on the town side, and as Stephen and Gilbert drew closer, some washing on a line strung between two trees.

"It seems the bridge has occupants," Gilbert said. People living under the town's bridges was a perennial problem. Last winter, squatters had built a fire under the Galdeford Bridge which had set part of it ablaze. The town elders had resolved that this sort of thing should not be permitted because of the danger, but the bailiffs had not been able to stop the practice entirely. As soon as they chased one group away another took its place.

Stephen quickened his pace. "Maybe they saw something."

"If they had, don't you think they'd have dug it up?"

"You are questioning me again."

"You have not yet won the bet."

They came abreast of the mill yard and were about to turn onto Dinham Road when Stephen stopped short and stood looking at the mill.

"What is it?" Gilbert asked.

"Someone I recognize."

"Why the odd look? You've lived here long enough to recognize quite a few people."

"This is someone I had not expected to see again."

Stephen strode through the gate. Three figures turned in his direction. "Dogface, Greg, Michael," Stephen called to them. "It's a surprise to run into you here."

"We was just passing through," Dogface said, a hand on the pommel of his sword. "Asking after a bit of bread, we was."

"Passing through?"

"On our way to greener pastures, what with Lord Richard dead, and all. We've no regular employment. We thought to find a more suitable place for ourselves."

"Lord Hugh —" Hugh de Tuberville constable of Montgomery castle "— didn't want you to stay on? They were shorthanded at Old Montgomery, after all."

"He had some such idea, but we didn't relish what he proposed to pay."

"I see. And Michael," Stephen said, "we've a score yet to settle."

"Can't you let it go?" Dogface asked. "He's a hot-headed lad, always losing his temper over this and that. Can't you let bygones lie?"

"I might," Stephen said, "but what's he doing with that shovel?"

Michael held a shovel, which he was trying to conceal behind his back.

"You're not planning to dig up what Melmerby stole, by any chance? Is that why you pushed him off in the tower? So you wouldn't have to share?"

Dogface's mouth writhed as he struggled to find a suitable reply, but what came out of his mouth was a snarl. "Get him, boys!"

"You're sure?" Greg said, hand going to his sword.

"He knows!" Dogface snapped. "Get him, or we're done for!"

They all drew swords. Greg and Michael raised theirs and came at Stephen, who had no sword, having left his at the inn, the wearing of swords about the town being a violation of local law. Dogface turned to the spectators in the yard to keep an eye on them so they wouldn't interfere; a good precaution because a couple of the men were about to reach into their wagons for their quarterstaffs.

The next moments seemed to take an eternity, as if time had slowed down. Stephen backed away, since running was out of the question — they were certain to catch him if he turned his back — momentarily at a loss about what to do. It was bad enough to face two swordsmen when you had a sword yourself, but certain death when all you had was a dagger. He might have drawn his dagger and done what little he could with that, but he might give Greg and Michael some warning that he knew what to do with it against a sword; such an apprehension could make them cautious and that would be the end of him. Instead he drew off his cloak and wrapped it twice around his left arm, yet leaving a length hanging, while giving ground until he had almost reached the wicker fence surrounding the yard, trying to look as helpless as possible.

Then they were upon him.

Michael came slightly ahead of Greg, on Stephen's left. As Michael struck a great downward blow, a rictus of effort contorting his face, Stephen took up the dangling end of his cloak with his right hand and slipped to the left. He raised the fabric overhead in the high shield and deflected Michael's blade to his right. This caused his left hand to wrap around the blade, catching the sword in a coil of fabric, but his right hand was free and he punched Michael in the throat.

Michael went "Gawk!" and let go of the sword and staggered backward, making choking noises. He sat down hard, hands at his throat, face beginning to change hue.

Stephen's sidestep put Michael between him and Greg. But as Michael stumbled backward, Stephen circled to use him as an obstacle for a few moments while he got hold of the sword. Now that he had a proper weapon, Stephen felt a little better about his chances as he settled into the low guard, sword by his right leg, point toward the ground, a deceptive guard that made a swordsman look vulnerable, but a guard full of menace.

Greg came on with a thrust that seemed wild and furious. Stephen set it aside with a low hanger that flowed into a downward cut at the head as he pivoted his body to the right. But Greg had anticipated this; he was not so new at swordplay after all. He parried the cut with the turned around hand, fist close to his left shoulder, knuckles up, point in the air; which put him in the perfect position for another thrust. Stephen knew it was coming, however, for this was a standard response he had practiced a thousand times, and he swept it away with his cloaked left arm.

Stephen's parry had given him a grasp of Greg's blade, a dangerous position for Greg, but rather than come to grips, Greg delivered a powerful front kick with his heel. If it had struck on Stephen's stomach the fight might have been over, but fortunately it connected with Stephen's hip, and though hard and painful, it only drove Stephen backward. He knew he could not prevent a fall, so he relaxed and took it, curling into a ball and rolling to his feet, glad there was nothing in the way.

Greg tried to take advantage of Stephen's fall by rushing forward with a great cut to the crown of his head. Stephen managed to raise his sword in time to parry it. He responded with downward cut of his own, but rather than stand and parry, Greg stepped back out of the way.

"For God's sake, Dog!" Greg cried. "Help me finish him! We haven't the time to waste!"

Dogface hesitated a moment. But the threat from the bystanders had abated, two of them running up hill toward the gate shouting about the affray and the remainder content to stand about and watch without interfering. So Dogface sheathed his sword and took up one of the quarterstaffs.

This put Stephen in a very bad position. In a fight even just one-to-one the man with the quarterstaff had the advantage over a swordsman, and here there were two of them.

Stephen was about to vault the wicker fence at his back to get away when Gilbert came round one of the carts and tackled Dogface from behind. Greg, taken aback by this unexpected interference, glanced at the two now scuffling in the dirt. At that instant, Greg's attention was not on Stephen and he attacked with a furious cut to Greg's left ear. Greg saw it coming out of the corner of his eye and he raised his sword again in the turned-around hand to parry. But Stephen's cut was a falsing, for he spun into a cut at Greg's right ear before the swords had a chance to clash. Greg was not quick enough to parry this one, and Stephen's sword cut diagonally through his head from just above the ear to the lower jaw. The top of Greg's head came free and fell to the ground like a hat knocked off. The partly headless body stood for a moment, the lower teeth and tongue visible and moving. Then Greg collapsed.

As Stephen turned to aid Gilbert, Dogface rose to his knees and punched Gilbert in the face, knocking him flat. Dogface's eyes swept the yard, taking in the bodies of Michael and Greg. He dashed to one of the horses, vaulted aboard, and galloped out of the yard. Stephen watched as he crossed the Dinham Bridge and continued up the road until a stand of willows by the river cut off the view.

Stephen helped Gilbert to his feet. "I wondered where you had got to."

"Have I broken anything?" Gilbert asked, hands to his face as if assuring himself it was still there, although not all in one piece perhaps.

"I don't think so, though you're going to have a devil of a shiner before the day is over."

"Oh, dear."

"Let's be glad that's the worst we've suffered over this," Stephen said, thinking with trepidation of the recriminations he would have to endure from Edith when they got back to the inn, and about how close the whole thing had been.

"Am I going to hear a thank you for my valiant effort?" Gilbert asked.

"Let's settle our bet first."

Stephen picked up the shovel that Michael had dropped.

"Hey," the miller protested. "That's mine."

Stephen said nothing and the miller added, "Why would you need a shovel?"

"What does anyone do with shovels? To dig up something."

"What's going on?"

"We're looking for something."

The miller glanced at the sword still in Stephen's hand. "Would you mind putting that down, sir? It makes me nervous."

"Ah, yes, certainly," Stephen said. He tossed the sword in the direction of Greg's body. "Leave everything as you see it. I expect the deputy sheriff will be displeased if anything is disturbed."

"Of course, sir. I wouldn't think of tidying up my yard."

"Gilbert," Stephen said, "let's get busy before Henle arrives to make trouble."

Gilbert searched the far bank of the river while Stephen took the near one, but neither of them spotted what might have been evidence of a recently dug hole. Stephen even looked into the lean-to made of branches and scrap wood the people living under the bridge had erected, but still he saw no sign. Gilbert returned from his search and they stood together under the bridge, gazing at the swift flow of the river.

"Henle will be here soon," Gilbert said, a palm over his injured eye which had begun to swell shut. "It's a good thing he's such a sluggard or he'd've been here already."

"Lucky for us. You'll have to keep looking when he gets here." Stephen was about to hand Gilbert the shovel and give up the search, or at least his part of it, when a little girl in the squatter family, which had watched these proceedings warily, threw a handful of twigs on the fire to keep it going. "There is one place we haven't looked."

"Where's that?" Gilbert asked.

But Stephen did not reply. "How long have you been here?" he asked the father of the squatter family.

"Ten days, maybe, sir," the man answered. "We came the same day that dead fellow was discovered at the castle."

"Ten days. And no one was here when you came?"

"No. People had been here before us, but the miller said it had been a week since the bailiffs had driven them off."

"I see," Stephen murmured, still gazing at the fire. He dug into the fire, which was surrounded by a circle of stones and tossed the flaming wood and coals aside. Then he dug down into the circle. He had got down a couple of feet and was about to give up when the shovel deposited a leather purse atop the pile of soil he had created. Stephen knelt and loosened the drawstrings. He upended the purse. Four large green stones in gold fittings fell out onto his palm. He held out the stones for Gilbert to see. "Look."

"Aaah!" Gilbert cried. He snatched the shovel and began throwing dirt every which way, deepening the hole. "It's not here! Saint Milburga's relic — it's not here!"

"No," Stephen said, "and I don't think we're going to find it, either."

Chapter 22

Voices on the road told Stephen that Walter Henle had arrived. Stephen emerged from beneath the bridge to face him. It would do no good to run away.

"Attebrook," Henle said with some satisfaction at the sight of him, "it looks like you've been up to some mischief."

"There was a spot of trouble here, but it's over now."

"I'm going to have to arrest you, you know."

Stephen had been expecting this. Homicide was homicide and punishable even if committed in self-defense. Only a pardon would save him, and those were expensive and hard to get. "Pesky thing, the law. Always forcing you to do things you don't want to do."

"Oh, I don't mind doing this. You've had it coming."

"I like it when a man enjoys his work so."

"Yes, I must admit, it does give me some pleasure to think of you in my gaol. Take him away, boys," Henle said to the deputies at his back. "Be sure that he's especially comfortable. I will be along shortly to see how he's doing."

Stephen was in hold for three weeks when the Prince returned from Wales with only his entourage, the army having been disbanded, victorious it was said, even if it hadn't fought a single battle. However, the Prince had relieved several castles in the north that had been besieged, and apparently that was reckoned enough for him to turn his attention to the more immediate threat to the crown: the discontent among many of the barons and the threat of civil war posed by Simon de Montfort's faction. He had been recalled to London for a council about how to address this threat.

The second day the Prince was in residence, a pair of castle wardens fetched Stephen from the gaol and escorted him to the hall, even though he was as bearded, unkept, and filthy by now as any denizen residing beneath one of Ludlow's bridges.

A person so filthy had no business in the hall, so Stephen wasn't surprised that he was made to wait at the foot of the stairs, although he could have done with not being chained to a post there.

"Sorry, sir," one of the wards, a fellow named Rodney, said. "Orders."

"Nowhere to run in here," Stephen said.

"Well, that thief, whoever he was, managed to get out. They reckon you're smarter than him, I suppose."

"But not smarter than you, and I know you'll keep a sharp eye on me."

"Oh, I'll do that. You can count on it."

About half an hour later, Sir Geoffrey Randall emerged and clumped down the steps with the help of a cane and the bannister. He looked up at Stephen, eyes a little rummy, his face a bit more careworn.

"Foot bothering you again, sir?" Stephen asked.

"Yes, dammit. What's the matter with you, boy? Why does trouble seem to rear its head whenever you're about?"

"Well, I thought I had solved the trouble, at least partly, anyway."

Sir Geoffrey nodded. "Yes, you've found the stones. But all these bodies lying about. Good God, what's happening to Ludlow? It was such a quiet, peaceful place until you showed up. Precious little for me to do, except for the occasional accident. Now I'm busy all the time!"

"Sorry, sir. But none of it's my doing — well, most of it, anyway."

"About those fellows at the mill. You're sure they were the culprits?"

"Most of them. Not the ringleader, I think. That was a fellow named Melmerby."

"One of Parfet's men, Gilbert said."

"Yes."

"And there's but one left alive to be brought to justice."

"That's my thought."

"I doubt we'll ever catch him. He'll go to ground, change his name, that sort of thing, if he's got any sense at all." Sir Geoffrey wagged a finger in Stephen's face. "But what are we to do with you, eh?"

"I had thought that since I was doing service for the crown that a pardon would be in order. You did speak to the Prince about that, I hope?"

"I exchanged some words with him to that effect. He is most pleased with the recovery of the gems, though his heart aches at the thought of the relic still out there. What became of it, do you think?"

"I imagine that the thieves tossed it in the river. I doubt they had much use for it. The stones were their objective all along."

"Stupid fellows."

"About that pardon, sir. What did the Prince say? He had mentioned a reward."

"Owing to the fact that you did not recover the relic, I doubt there will be a reward."

"Oh," Stephen said, crushed. "Not even a little one?"

"Not even a little one. As for a pardon, a gift might hasten it."

"You wouldn't by any chance be able to lend me some money, would you, sir?"

"Lend you money? You are daft, boy. No, but you have a fine horse. The Prince would be satisfied with that, I'm sure."

Stephen was dismayed. No doubt Sir Geoffrey meant his war horse. The stallion was worth a lot of money. He was the last thing Stephen hoped to part with. "How sure are you, sir?"

"We spoke about it. FitzAllen argued against it, of course. He thinks you ought to hang, you know, and he makes quite a persuasive argument for it. But the Prince seemed receptive to a pardon, despite FitzAllen's meddling and accusations against you, once I mentioned that stallion of yours. If you are amenable, I shall tell him."

"Don't let me keep you, sir. I know that standing on your bad foot is a trial."

Sir Geoffrey harumphed, and went back upstairs.

He came back out in another quarter hour. This time he remained at the top of the steps. "You fellows can let him go!" he called down to the castle wardens. "He's been bailed, on the Prince's order."

"Stephen, my dear fellow," Sir Geoffrey continued as the wardens fussed with the manacles, "the Prince has decided to give the stones to the monastery at Greater Wenlock, for their continued prayers and all that. It's a most happy resolution all round, don't you think?"

"Happy, yes, I am happy everything turned out so well." Stephen rubbed his wrists where the manacles had chafed.

"Good, then," Sir Geoffrey said. "What are you waiting for? Off you go." He turned back into the hall.

"Bit of bad luck, losing your best horse like that, sir," Rodney, the guard, said.

"It's a fucking disaster." Honor and dignity required that he show no feeling, but he was so distraught at having lost the one thing above all others that marked him as a knight and a man of position, if not substance, that the words escaped his tongue before he could recall them. At least Sir Geoff had gone inside and could not see or hear him disgrace himself. "I'll never be able to afford another like him. Nor get away from this place."

The Prince dispatched a priest from his entourage to carry the stones to Greater Wenlock and deliver his conditions for the bequest. Stephen heard about this from Harry as they shared a tub at the Wobbly Kettle, although Harry had been reluctant to do so since Stephen was so filthy.

"I'll never get my own grime off, what with all that's come off you!" Harry had protested. But since there were no other free tubs at the time, due to all the custom the Kettle was getting from the men-at-arms of the Prince's household, he had no choice. Besides, Stephen was paying, and Harry would not refuse charity, regardless of its form.

Gilbert, meanwhile, sat on a bench, sipping wine, as he had no desire to share a tub with Harry no matter how much he needed a bath himself. He leaned against the wall, face long, which was a feat owing to its naturally round condition.

"What's the matter with you?" Stephen asked Gilbert when he noticed Gilbert's sad expression.

"Yes," Harry said, "what have you been up to? He never looks that way except when he's feeling guilty about something."

"I'm not feeling guilty about anything," Gilbert protested. "But I am troubled."

"Troubled about what?" Stephen asked.

"I'd rather not say." It was clear from Gilbert's tone that he was reluctant to speak of whatever bothered him before Harry, who might be prone both to needle him about it and spread the word to the rest of Ludlow and beyond.

Harry swam to the near side of the tub, hands on either side of his face, only his nose and above showing. "This sounds serious. Cheated on Edith, have you?"

"I have not!" Gilbert said indignantly.

"That's a relief. I was worried about that," Harry said.

"It is," Gilbert allowed at long last, "about my book."

"What book?" Harry asked. "I didn't know you fancied literature."

"You are a man without the slightest bit of culture, nor conscience, I might add, after all the trouble you've caused Jennie," Gilbert said. "I would not expect you to understand."

"Your book," Stephen murmured. He knew exactly what Gilbert meant: his purloined Gospel, the one he had taken when he left Greater Wenlock.

"I've been thinking — you shut up!" Gilbert pointed a finger at Harry, whose mouth had opened to speak. "I don't want to hear a word from you!"

Harry subsided in the tub at the fury of this outcry, content to wait and see what revelation would ensure.

Gilbert went on, rubbing the bench with his fingers. "I've been thinking I should return it. For my soul."

Harry started to comment again, but Stephen laid a hand on his shoulder and forestalled whatever he planned to say. Stephen said, "We should ride up there then."

"I suppose we should," Gilbert said.

It was only twenty miles from Ludlow to Greater Wenlock, but it took most of the day to get there, owing to Gilbert's mule, whose fastest pace was a slow walk unless it was startled by something, but being an unusually level-headed and stubborn mule, it could not be coaxed nor startled into going any faster. This was just as well, since Gilbert was liable to fall off at any more energetic pace.

It was late afternoon when they finally arrived, and the fields about the town had already begun to clear as people gave thought to supper.

The priory lay to the east of the town, and it was a pleasant sight, a neat, modest abbey flanked by timber buildings on the south side forming the priory close. A groom offered to put up their horses, but Stephen declined, saying, "Thank you, but we will take a room in the town."

Gilbert paused at the passage into the cloister, lips pursed.

"If you burst into tears, I'll give you a clout," Stephen said.

"Just remembering things, is all."

"Happy memories?"

"For the most part. Hard work, hard prayer, strict obedience. I loved it for all that."

"It is hard to imagine you being strict about anything."

"Well, I did get in a lot of trouble about that. Brother Anthony always had to get after me. I suppose he found me exasperating."

"These reminiscences are all well and good, but my stomach is growling. You finished Edith's ham and cheese hours ago, and left me little part."

"I have more to feed that you do." Gilbert released the leather case he clutched to his round stomach to give the stomach a pat.

They entered the cloister and crossed to the refectory, passing a stone-walled well. A servant asked what they wanted, and having heard their desires, delivered a message to Prior Anthony. The servant returned in short order to escort them to the prior's chamber.

Prior Anthony received them in a high-backed chair, looking more worn and stooped than he had only a few weeks ago. Brother Adolphus stood at Prior Anthony's side.

"Sir Stephen," Prior Anthony said in his reedy voice which one had to strain to hear, "what a surprise to see you. We understand that we have you to thank for the return of the emeralds. We are so grateful for that small bit of fortune."

"*We* found them," Stephen said, indicating Gilbert.

"Yes. Master Wistwode. I must say I had not expected to see you again. Is there some special reason for your visit?" Prior Anthony's eyes lingered on the leather case, which was large enough to contain a large book.

Gilbert coughed. He was about to speak, but Stephen held up a hand to stop him.

"He has business with you. But so do I. I should like that taken care of first."

"Your business?" Prior Anthony asked. "What business could you have with us?"

"I want you to fetch the relic. I want to see it."

"Whatever are you talking about?" Brother Adolphus burst out. "It was stolen!"

"It was stolen, but not by the men who took the stones."

"Stephen!" Gilbert cried. "What are you saying?"

"I have been thinking this long day, and I have finally worked it out," Stephen said. "When Ormyn Yarker climbed into the storeroom at the chapel and took up the relic, he pried the stones from the bones. He had not come for the bones and did not care about them. Or perhaps he feared spiritual retribution if he took the relics. I don't know. In any case, he left them behind, along with parts of the clasps." He held out the small golden clasp he had found in the relic's box the day of his examination. "In the morning, one of your order opened the box and discovered that the stones were missing. You then saw your opportunity to seize the relic for yourselves by claiming it had been taken as well. You thought that the thieves would never be found and people would think the relic lost forever. But you had it safe."

"That is a scurrilous accusation!" Brother Adolphus cried.

He was about to protest more, but Prior Anthony held up a hand. "Adolphus," he said with resignation, "it seems we have been found out, after all." Anthony addressed Stephen, "I pray before the relic every day for the saint's guidance and help. That morning when I opened the box, the bones indeed were there, although the stones," and his voice hardened here at mention of the stones, "were not, thank God. Although we had thought the adornment of the relic was a sacrilege, I then realized it was part of the saint's plan to put her remains into the hands of those who love her most, those who do not seek to profit by her but to do good and her will. Our saint will be safe here, out of the hands of that man, FitzAllen."

"Thank God!" Gilbert said.

"Thank God, indeed," Adolphus said.

"Bring it out," Stephen said.

"What good would that do?" Anthony asked. "You have my confession. Is that not enough for you?"

"Bring it out so that Gilbert can see it."

"Stephen," Gilbert said, "I don't need to really."

"Be quiet, Gilbert."

Anthony's fingers drummed on the arm of his chair. "Brother Adolphus, would you be so kind as to fetch Saint Milburga's bones?"

"Brother Anthony —" Adolphus protested.

"Please!" Anthony said. "Let us indulge this young man. He is the law, so I suppose he has a right to see the stolen goods."

"This is a mistake," Adolphus said, despite the prior's order. But after a moment, he retreated to another chamber.

Adolphus returned bearing a small, plain wooden cask. He gave the cask to Anthony, who rested it in his lap and tilted up the lid. The remains of a human thigh, brown and aged, lay within the box, in three pieces now rather than two.

"It's been damaged," Gilbert said in a voice tinged with awe and pain.

"So it has," Anthony said, "but it is still Saint Milburga nonetheless."

"What now?" Anthony asked Stephen. "Will you report your discovery to the Prince? I understand that you are in some trouble with the law."

"I just wished to be sure," Stephen said. "You have a complaint about a trespass done to you years ago. Charity requires that you forgive it, and let it rest where things lie. I would have that done."

Anthony glanced again at the leather case in Gilbert's hands, eyes shrewd, as if he already knew what it contained. He nodded. "God tells us to be charitable and forgiving."

"Good," Stephen said. "Thank you." He put a hand on Gilbert's shoulder. "We're done here."

"What?" Gilbert said, for his attention was still on the relic and he did not seem to have understood what had just happened.

"What will you do when you return to Ludlow?" Anthony asked. "What will you say?"

"Nothing," Stephen said. "We were never here."

Anthony smiled. "We are ever grateful."

"So are we."